ODD SQUAD
AGENT'S HANDBOOK

Agent O_____

[Imprint]
MAKE YOUR MARK

A part of Macmillan Publishing Group, LLC
120 Broadway, New York, NY 10271

ODD SQUAD AGENT'S HANDBOOK.™ The Fred Rogers Company.
© 2020 The Fred Rogers Company. All rights reserved. Printed in the
United States of America by LSC Communications, Harrisonburg, Virginia.

Library of Congress Control Number: 2019932732

ISBN 978-1-250-22266-4 (hardcover) / ISBN 978-1-250-22267-1 (ebook)

Our books may be purchased in bulk for promotional, educational, or
business use. Please contact your local bookseller or the Macmillan
Corporate and Premium Sales Department at (800) 221-7945 ext. 5442
or by email at MacmillanSpecialMarkets@macmillan.com.

Book design and illustrations by Jason Lean

Special thanks to Jeff Miller, Faceout Studios

Imprint logo designed by Amanda Spielman

First edition, 2020

10 9 8 7 6 5 4 3 2 1

mackids.com

Something very odd happens to those who steal books.
They will float off the ground, getting all sorts of looks.
Then they'll fly up through the trees,
Knocking branches with their knees.
And drift through the sky.
Until they turn into pie.

**FOR FRANNY
AND HENRY**

THIS PAGE INTENTIONALLY
LEFT BLANK EXCEPT FOR THESE WORDS
YOU ARE READING RIGHT NOW.

Okay, fine. These words, too.

ODD SQUAD
AGENT'S HANDBOOK

TIM MCKEON AND ADAM PELTZMAN

{Imprint}
MAKE YOUR MARK

New York

TABLE OF CONTENTS

Letter from Ms. O 2

How to Make a Bookmark for this Book 5

Other Way to Make a Bookmark for this Book 6

SECTION I: WELCOME TO ODD SQUAD

Odd Squad Mission Statement 7

The Odd Squad Anthem 8

Odd Squad Oath 10

How to Tell the Difference Between the Odd Squad Mission Statement,
the Odd Squad Anthem, the Odd Squad Oath, and Bighorn Sheep 12

UNIT II: WORDS & PICTURES TO KNOW

The Odd Squad Seal 14

How to Catch a Jackalope 16

Glossary of Common Odd Squad Words 17

Odd Squad Symbols and Their Meanings 20

SECTOR III: A HISTORY OF ODD SQUAD

Famous Moments in Odd Squad History 24

Timeline of the Odd Squad Organization 26

Famous People in Odd Squad History 28

STAGE IV: GUIDE TO HEADQUARTERS

The Bullpen 31

The Ball Pit 34

The Hall of Doors 36

The Break Room 39

The Laboratory 40

SEGMENT V: YOUR UNIFORM & OTHER THINGS YOU WEAR

A Guide to Your Uniform 42

Are You Wearing Your Uniform Correctly? 44

Secret Suit Functions 45

Official Uniform Functions 46

How to Tie Your Tie 47

Replacement Uniforms 48

Reasons for Replacement Uniforms 50

Your Badge Number 51

How to Use Your Badge Phone 52

How to Use Your Watch Tablet 56

PORTION VI: GADGETS

The Almost Impossible-to-Use Gadget 60

Gadget Sign-Out Sheet 62

A Guide to Commonly Used Gadgets 66

A Guide to Uncommonly Used Gadgets 68

How to Combine Gadgets 70

Odd Squad Apple Pie Recipe 72

VIITH INNING STRETCH: YOUR PARTNER

Get to Know Your Partner 79

When Nothing Odd Is Happening 81

HENRY THE VIII: ODD CREATURES

Classification of Creatures 84

What to Do If You Are Slimed by a Blob 86

How to Interrogate a Unicorn 88

ALLOTMENT IX: ODD DISEASES

List of Common Odd Diseases 92

DIVISION X: ODD VILLAINS & FLOATING SANDWICHES

Floating Sandwiches 97

PORTION XI: WHEN SOMETHING VERY ODD HAS HAPPENED

What Seems to Be the Problem? 100

What's Odd with This Picture? 102

Form 0-135 104

SERIES XII: WHY ORCHID? WHY NOW? ORCHID NOW

We Interrupt This Book 106

CHUNK XIII: TUBE TRAVEL

How to Ride in the Tubes 112

Tips for Nervous Tube Travelers 115

Frequent Adverbs Used to Describe Tube Travel 116

Infrequent Adverbs Used to Describe Tube Travel 116

How to Find Tube Entrances. 117

Should I Tube Travel? 119

EPISODE XIV: FITNESS & NUTRITION

Coach O's Exercises to Stay Fit. 123

Oksana's Guide to Nutrition 127

Odd Squad Menu 128

Pros and Cons of Potatoes 130

BATCH XV: WORKPLACE SAFETY

Odd Squad Headquarters Safety Hazards 134

Watch Out for Each Other 136

Safe Vs. Unsafe 138

SWEET XVI: QUESTIONS & ANSWERS

Frequently Asked Questions About Odd Squad 141

Infrequently Asked Questions About Odd Squad 143

Odd Squad Holidays Observed 145

Goodbye Letter from Ms. O 147

Appendix 149

A Page in Ancient Jackalopian 150

Publisher's Note from Agent Omorro. 151

LETTER FROM MS. O

Welcome to Odd Squad and congratulations on joining the best kid-run organization on Earth and the second-best kid-run organization outside of Earth. I hope you will enjoy being an agent just as much as I did back when I was Agent Oprah.

Soon you will be assigned to work at one of the many Odd Squad precincts located across the world. Who knows? Maybe you'll be picked to work with me at Odd Squad Precinct #13579. If so, please bring me a juice box. Here are some juice flavors that I like:

OFFICIAL FLAVORS OF JUICE FOR MS. O

○ Apple   ○ Orange

○ CranApple   ○ CranGrape

○ Grape   ○ Pineapple

○ CranAppleCranPeachCranOrange-CranGrapeCranPineappleApple

○ Any Other Flavor Whatsoever

1 + 1 = 2

This handbook will explain everything you need to know to be the best agent possible. Maybe you think you know everything and don't need to read this book. Maybe you think this book would be better used as a doorstop or a very small step stool. Or maybe you are thinking about grinding it up into paste and adding hot water to make book oatmeal.

Think again.

There is stuff in here that they don't teach at Odd Squad Academy. I know because I went to the academy. Yes, that was over a hundred years ago and, no, I will not tell you how old I am. To sum up: Read the book. Don't fight oddness until you do. Turn the pages carefully so you don't get paper cuts.

Well, what are you waiting for?
Go . . . turn the page.

With appreciation,

MS. O

Ms. O (dictated but not read)

4 - 1 = 3

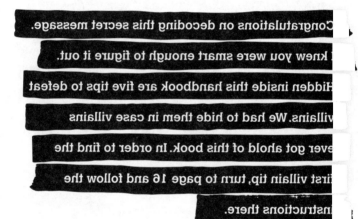

Congratulations on decoding this secret message.

I knew you were smart enough to figure it out.

Hidden inside this handbook are five tips to defeat

villains. We had to hide them in case villains

ever got ahold of this book. In order to find the

first villain tip, turn to page 16 and follow the

instructions there.

2 twice = 4

HOW TO MAKE A BOOKMARK FOR THIS BOOK

STEP 1: Make friends with a lumberjack.

STEP 2: Ask the lumberjack to cut down a tree. If the lumberjack says no, try again, but this time say please. Lumberjacks appreciate that.

STEP 3: Take the raw wood from the tree to a paper processing plant. If you don't know where to find a paper processing plant, you may need to build your own.

STEP 4: Use the machines at the plant to turn the wood into pulp.

STEP 5: Leave the wet pulp out to dry.

STEP 6: Meanwhile, gather metal to make scissors and plastic to make scissor handles.

STEP 7: Grind, polish, and assemble your scissors.

STEP 8: Use finished scissors to cut out dried paper pulp in the shape of a rectangle. A rectangle has four straight sides and four right angles. We suggest making two sides longer than the other two.

1st odd number after 4 = 5

OTHER WAY TO MAKE A BOOKMARK FOR THIS BOOK

STEP 1: Use scissors you already have and cut out the thing below.

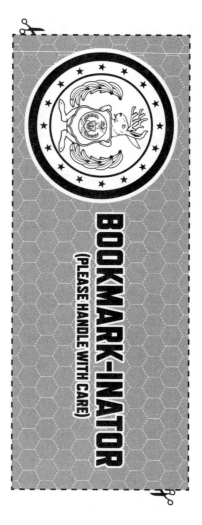

BOOKMARK-INATOR
(PLEASE HANDLE WITH CARE)

1 + 1 + 1 + 1 + 1 + 1 = 6

WELCOME TO ODD SQUAD

Top Secret: Odd Squad is not a secret. If someone sees you blasting a gadget or whooshing out of a tube entrance, it's all cool. You don't need to use the mind-erase-inator or anything. If someone has questions about Odd Squad, feel free to answer them. Maybe in a funny voice because who doesn't like funny voices?

If someone asks what Odd Squad does, you can read the official Odd Squad Mission Statement listed below. Because it is official, feel free to read it in an official voice:

ODD SQUAD
MISSION STATEMENT
**To investigate anything strange,
weird, and especially odd.
To put things right again.**

7 + 1 - 1 = 7

THE ODD SQUAD ANTHEM

OLIVER OCTAVIUS OLIVANDER 1893

Put a belt on 0 = 8

Every morning at every Odd Squad headquarters begins with agents singing the Odd Squad Anthem. "Anthem" is a fancy word we use for "song" because we just do. Scientists should sing the low notes, and Tube Operators should sing the high notes. Everyone else can sing however they want.

Once the anthem is over, congratulate your fellow agents on their excellent singing voices. Now it is time to read the Odd Squad Oath. The oath is a set of rules that every agent agrees to follow.

When saying the oath, agents should place one hand on their head and their other hand on their belly. If agents have additional hands, please make them shake each other.

$3 + 3 + 3 = 9$

ODD SQUAD OATH

I, **Agent O**_____,

do hereby:

⬡ Pledge to do no odd.

⬡ Pledge to stop any oddness from causing harm
or being just really, really annoying to any person,
place, or thing.

⬡ Pledge to do my job as fast as I can unless I am
caught in a time loop. Unless I am caught in a
time loop.

⬡ Pledge to treat each client with kindness and respect,
but especially anyone named Mysetereipolisxilpocky,
because Mysetereipolisxilpocky is a tough name to
say and spell and Mysetereipolisxilpocky probably
has to spend a lot of time correcting people and that
can't be fun for Mysetereipolisxilpocky.

⬡ Pledge to always ask my partner for help when I
need it.

9 + 1 = 10

○ Pledge to take breaks in the middle of lists of pledges like this one. Break suggestion: Read another list entitled "List of Break Suggestions for Taking Breaks in the Middle of Lists." But also take a break in the middle of that list.

○ Pledge to always help my partner whenever they need help.

○ Pledge to use a gadget when needed and not to use a gadget when not needed because that's show-offy.

○ Pledge to no longer make oaths that sound fancy and official, for they can be quite confusing, and no person nor place nor thing knows what I am even talking about anymore, henceforth and heretofore for thine own last words be true.

lowest number that rhymes with 7 = 11

HOW TO TELL THE DIFFERENCE BETWEEN THE ODD SQUAD MISSION STATEMENT, THE ODD SQUAD ANTHEM, THE ODD SQUAD OATH, AND BIGHORN SHEEP

We know. It's a lot of information to remember. Especially early in the morning. For that reason, below is a chart so you can quickly tell the difference between the Odd Squad Mission Statement, Odd Squad Anthem, and Odd Squad Oath. This chart will also stop you from mixing up any of the three with a bighorn sheep.

	📄 Mission Statement	♪♪♪ Anthem	🖋 Oath	🐏 Bighorn Sheep
Singable	✗	✗		
Short and Sweet	✗	✗		
Long and Sour			✗	
Lives in Alpine Meadows				✗
Battery Powered				
Has Horns			✗	✗

4 + 4 + 5 - 1 = 12

UNIT

II

WORDS & PICTURES TO KNOW

We guess you already know words like "we" and "guess" and "you" and "already" and "know" and "words" and "like." If not, you wouldn't have gotten through that first sentence and made it to this one.

That's great you know all those words, but there are new words and pictures you must learn to do your job as an Odd Squad agent. If you have a fear of learning new words, that is called sophophobia. But look! You just learned the word sophophobia, didn't you? And that wasn't so bad, was it? We think you're going to do great.

The **ODD SQUAD SEAL** is a picture used to represent
the Odd Squad organization. If you see this on something,
that something belongs to Odd Squad.

140 if you remove the 0 = 14

WHY A CIRCLE?

The artist hired to draw the seal, Agent Origami, tried to draw a square. Unfortunately, Origami had a hard time drawing corners and straight lines.

WHY SIXTEEN STARS?

These are sixteen reminders that every member of Odd Squad is a star.

WHY EIGHTEEN BANANAS?

Because Agent Origami felt that seventeen bananas were not quite enough potassium.

WHY THE JACKALOPE?

The jackalope was the first odd creature spotted by an Odd Squad agent. As a result, it became the official mascot. It was later discovered that jackalopes could speak. Common sayings include: "To be continued" and "Now, the rest of the story."

WHY IS THE JACKALOPE HOLDING A SHIELD?

Jackalopes always hold shields to protect themselves from falling meteors.

WHY ARE THERE ENDLESS JACKALOPES INSIDE THE SHIELD?

There are an endless number of jackalopes in the world. We are just trying to be correct.

HOW TO CATCH A JACKALOPE

Jackalopes. Let's face it, our jobs would be much easier without them. It seems like jackalopes wake up every morning and wonder how to mess things up for the rest of us. Has an entire street been covered in slime or jam or mashed potatoes? Well, you can bet a jackalope did it. Are things suddenly disappearing or moving backward or flattening for no reason? That has jackalope written all over it.

But just because a jackalope is sneaky and fast doesn't mean you can't catch one. And here's an important tip: Jackalopes always leave clues. Even if they don't mean to. Sometimes they strike in a pattern you can figure out. Sometimes they'll send you a message announcing their evil plans, and you can look for clues in the message.

Or sometimes, you can just follow their jackalope footprints. Right up to their secret jackalope lair. And there you'll find the jackalope, laughing its evil jackalope laugh, wearing its big jackalope hairdo, saying its jackalope catchphrase, and surrounded by all its jackalope friends. But there's nowhere for the jackalope to run. Thanks to you. So go ahead and enjoy your victory. Tell the jackalope, "Nice try, jackalope. You think you're so cute. But you can't outsmart Odd Squad. Busted."

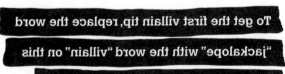

To get the first villain tip, replace the word "jackalope" with the word "villain" on this page. Turn to page 60 for the next tip.

16 - 0 = 16

GLOSSARY OF COMMON ODD SQUAD WORDS

Agent: Somebody who solves cases. Example: you.

Badge: Something you wear on your suit to show that you work at Odd Squad.

Badge Phone: A cellular phone that your badge can become when you open it. Please put it on silent during movies.

Big O: The head of the entire Odd Squad organization.

Bull pen: A device that a smart bull writes with.

Bullpen: The area of headquarters where agents work.

Case: *1.* An odd problem that needs to be solved. *2.* The thing you keep your pencils in.

Creature: An odd animal or beast. Often, but not always, hairy.

Gadget: A device used to help solve an odd problem.

Glossary: An alphabetical list of words and their definitions. Often found in a book like this one.

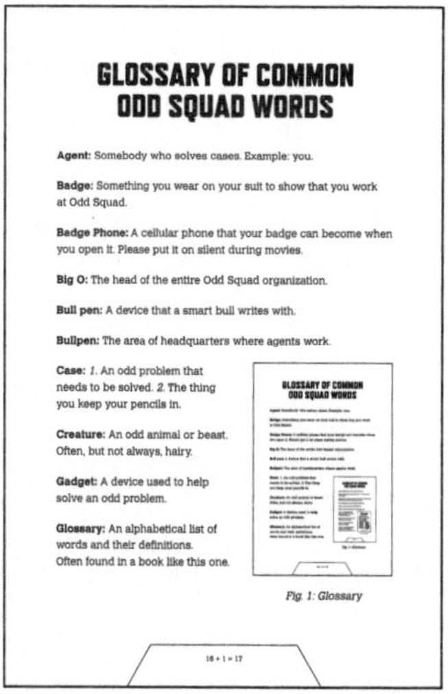
GLOSSARY OF COMMON ODD SQUAD WORDS
Agent: Somebody who solves cases. Example: you.
Badge: Something you wear on your suit to show that you work at Odd Squad.
Badge Phone: A cellular phone that your badge can become when you open it. Please put it on silent during movies.
Big O: The head of the entire Odd Squad organization.
Bull pen: A device that a smart bull writes with.
Bullpen: The area of headquarters where agents work.
Case: 1. An odd problem that needs to be solved. 2. The thing you keep your pencils in.
Creature: An odd animal or beast. Often, but not always, hairy.
Gadget: A device used to help solve an odd problem.
Glossary: An alphabetical list of words and their definitions. Often found in a book like this one.
Fig. 1: Glossary
16 + 1 = 17

Fig. 1: Glossary

Handbook: The book you are holding in your hands.

Headquarters: The place where Odd Squad agents work.

Jackalope: A jackrabbit with antelope horns. The official animal mascot of Odd Squad.

Lab: *1.* Where Odd Squad scientists work and where the gadgets are kept. *2.* Such a cute dog.

Medical Bay: Where the Odd Squad doctor works.

Medical Ocean: Not actually a thing.

Mission: Like a case, but a super-serious one that you should be all super serious about.

Mr. O: Your boss if your boss is a boy.

Ms. O: Your boss if your boss is a girl.

Fig. 2: Jackalope

Mssssssssss. O: Your boss if your boss is a girl snake (Precinct #97175 only).

Odd Squad: Well, you know, it's the whole thing that we're talking about here.

OSMU: The abbreviation for Odd Squad Mobile Unit. They also answer to their names: Opal, Omar, Oswald, and Orla.

6 + 6 + 6 = 18

Partner: An agent you are assigned to work with. He or she or they will watch out for you and help you be the best that you can possibly be. They have been known to become a lifelong friend.

Precinct: The place where your Odd Squad office is located. Each precinct has its own number.

Squishinating: What happens when you get squished into a ball to ride through the tubes.

Sqtng: What happens when the word *squishinating* gets squished into a ball to ride through the tubes.

Trophy Room: The place where old things from Odd Squad history are kept.

Tubes: What Odd Squad agents use to travel to anywhere in the world.

Uniform: The clothing worn by Odd Squad agents.

Villain: Somebody who makes odd things happen on purpose.

Vivian: A thirty-nine-year-old woman who made an odd thing happen by accident. It's okay. We fixed it.

Watch Tablet: A touchscreen that your wristwatch can expand to become. Also doubles as a plate to eat your lunch.

Zyx: A made-up word used to end a glossary.

$12 + 3 + 4 = 19$

ODD SQUAD SYMBOLS AND THEIR MEANINGS

Management

Investigation

Science

Medical

Maintenance and Tube Operation

Security

Internal Investigation

Creature Control

Fitness

15 + 58 - 53 = 20

Big O

Continuing
Kid Education

Obfusco

Leaky Faucet
Action Team B

Mobile Unit

Kitchen

Library

No Entry or a Cool
Ninja, Depending on
How You Look at It

Invisible Unit

20 and a ½ rounded up = 21

A HISTORY OF ODD SQUAD

Hey, guys. Oscar here. I'm the head historian at the Odd Squad Academy, and I'm going to talk about science! No, wait. That's not right. I'm the head scientist at the Odd Squad Academy, and I'm going to talk about history. Yes. That's it. Anyway, Ms. O said I know a lot about stuff, and so she asked me to talk a bit about some of the stuff that I know. So here we goooooo. Oops. The letter *O* key got stuck. Ha. That was kind of fun.

If you're going to be a great Odd Squad agent, it's important to know your history. Sometimes knowing about a case from a long time ago can help you solve a problem you're working on today. For example, one time I couldn't find my toothpick. Then I read a book all about a brave Odd Squad agent in medieval times named Sir Ollagher, who was trying to solve a case about a castle that was turned upside down. Well, it turns out my toothpick was saving my page in the book. See how that story helped me find my toothpick?

The point is, study up and get to know about the Odd Squad agents that came before you. I hope their stories inspire you to get out there, do great work, and make history, tooooooooooooooooooooooo. Oops. It happened again.

Scientifically speaking,

Oscar

Oscar

1 + 2 + 20 = 23

FAMOUS MOMENTS IN ODD SQUAD HISTORY

300 BC: GREAT WALL OF CHINA SHRINKS

When the Chinese emperor discovered that the Great Wall of China was shrunk down to six inches tall, he briefly renamed it the Not-So-Great Wall of China, and then he cried in his palace for forty days. Finally, he called Odd Squad, who tracked down who did it—a villain named Smallsy Wallsy. He agreed to hand over his shrink ray if Odd Squad promised to write about him one day in a history book. Fine, Smallsy. Happy now?

1503: MONA LISA RETURNED

Shortly after finishing his masterpiece, Leonardo da Vinci was alarmed to discover that Mona Lisa had escaped from the painting. He called Odd Squad, who found Mona Lisa at a nearby market. Since she was going to be in a painting for the rest of her life, she wanted to bring along a few things, like some snacks and a book of crossword puzzles. Legend has it that the agents helped her solve one of the crossword puzzles, which is why she is smiling in the painting.

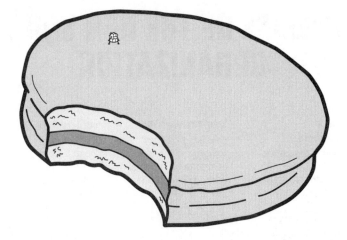

1969: MAN WALKS ON MOON PIE (ALMOST)

Neil Armstrong was about to become the first man to walk on the moon when he discovered that the moon had been turned into a dessert called a moon pie. Delicious, but not something you want to step in. Two Odd Squad agents were sent to the moon in an Odd Squad rocket to fix the problem. They hovered above the delicious moon and hit it with a blast from an un-moon-pie-inator gadget. Instantly, the moon transformed from a tasty treat to a dirty rock once more. Neil Armstrong became the first man to walk on the moon, while the Odd Squad agents became the first boy and girl to skip and jump rope on it.

5086: GALACTIC PALACE TURNED INTO TAN SOCKS

The ruler of the universe, a gerbil named Patty, will discover her Palace of Peace has been turned into a pair of tan socks. Odd Squad agents will materialize next to the socks and use their minds to rebuild the palace. **NOTE:** We know this will happen because we have time travel.

$5 + 5 + 5 + 5 + 5 = 25$

TIMELINE OF THE ODD SQUAD ORGANIZATION

66 Million BC (that afternoon)

Odd Squad organization formed with other caveboys and cavegirls.

Year 8 to Year 1850

Everyone so busy fighting oddness that everyone forgot about writing down stuff to put on the timeline.

February 3, 1876

First badge phone invented. It weighs forty-five pounds and must be plugged into the wall at all times.

66 Million BC (that afternoon) until the year 7

Many more triple peanuts discovered. It was mostly about peanuts for a while.

September 5, 1850, 5:19 P.M.

Agent O'Quill decides to add time of day to timeline.

March 23, 1882

Famous mathematician Emmy Noether born. Odd Squad becomes a big fan.

Year 8

First jackalopes reveal they can talk, and they show kids all the odd things they have been missing. Kids are grateful.

September 6, 1850

Agent O'Quill decides not to add time of day because it's a lot of work and feels really overwhelming. Agent O'Quill goes back to just month, day, and year.

November 11, 1927

Ms. O approached by the inventor of the television, Philo Taylor Farnsworth, to make a television program. Ms. O says no. She suggests, "Try again in eighty-seven years."

Year 7

First jackalopes discovered.

66 Million BC

Cavegirl named O discovers peanut shell with three peanuts inside; the first odd problem on record.

September 4, 1850

Agent O'Quill remembers the timeline and decides to add days and months to make it easier to read.

September 18, 1889

Odd Squad tube system invented by Big Red.

$$2 + 6 + 2 + 6 + 2 + 6 + 2 = 26$$

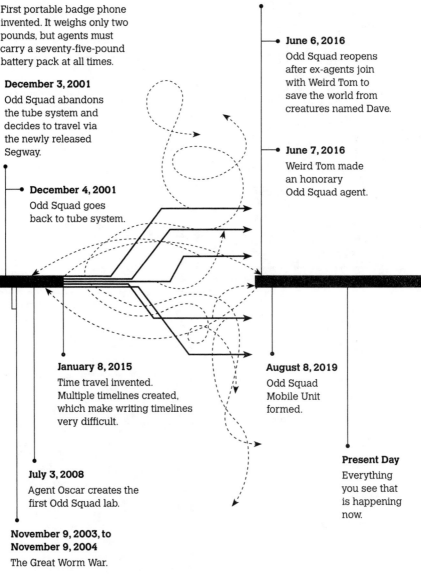

September 3, 1971
First video game "Space War!" created. Much, much less work gets done at Odd Squad.

May 8, 1987
First portable badge phone invented. It weighs only two pounds, but agents must carry a seventy-five-pound battery pack at all times.

December 3, 2001
Odd Squad abandons the tube system and decides to travel via the newly released Segway.

December 4, 2001
Odd Squad goes back to tube system.

May 6, 2016
Weird Tom sets up rival "Weird Team," causing Odd Squad to shut down.

June 6, 2016
Odd Squad reopens after ex-agents join with Weird Tom to save the world from creatures named Dave.

June 7, 2016
Weird Tom made an honorary Odd Squad agent.

January 8, 2015
Time travel invented. Multiple timelines created, which make writing timelines very difficult.

August 8, 2019
Odd Squad Mobile Unit formed.

July 3, 2008
Agent Oscar creates the first Odd Squad lab.

Present Day
Everything you see that is happening now.

November 9, 2003, to November 9, 2004
The Great Worm War.

FAMOUS PEOPLE IN ODD SQUAD HISTORY

AGENT ORVALSSON

A Viking agent from Norway, Orvalsson led many missions in the Odd Sea. Orvalsson was so tough that he was rumored to eat Hydroclopses for breakfast, until he got tired of them and switched over to cornflakes.

AGENT OTHENS

Winner of the first O Games, Othens was considered the greatest athlete in Odd Squad history. She once threw a javelin all the way from Greece to Little Rock, Arkansas.

AGENT O'TASSLE

Agent known for being the
fastest gadget drawer in
the West. Her drawings of
gadgets were not very good,
but they were the fastest.

AGENT OOFA

General in the Great Worm
War. Also famous for
looking exactly like Agent
O'Tassle, even though she
was not related in any way
whatsoever.

GUIDE TO HEADQUARTERS

An Odd Squad headquarters is so many things. It's your office. It's where you eat. It's where your friends are. It's where your pens are. It's where your friends' pens are. And if your pens are the friends of your friends' pens, then it's also where your friends' pens' pen friends are.

But headquarters can be tough to figure out. There are so many rooms, hallways, odd creatures, departments, employees, and places to hang up your hat. Did you know there are over two hundred hat hooks in a typical Odd Squad headquarters? Which is odd, because hats are not part of the uniform.

The good news is every Odd Squad headquarters is pretty much the same.* After reading the next few pages, you'll be able to visit any Odd Squad in the world and know what is what. You won't have to ask embarrassing questions like, "Where's the creature room in this place?" and "If I had a hat, would there be any place for me to hang it?"

*The only Odd Squad that isn't the same is the one in the Arctic. The Mr. O up there does his own thing, and we respect that.

10 + 10 + 10 = 30

THE BULLPEN

The bullpen is what we call the open space in the middle of headquarters. This is where your desk and your partner's desk will be. You will share your desk with a night-shift agent who comes to work when the sun goes down. Don't worry about emptying all the drawers and cleaning all your stuff off every night to make room. Each night, maintenance agents destroy everything inside and on top of your desk, then rebuild and replace it with exact copies in time for morning.

Since you will be spending a lot of time in the bullpen, you should feel free to decorate your desk in a way that makes you happy. Turn the page to see some examples of how other agents have decorated their desks.

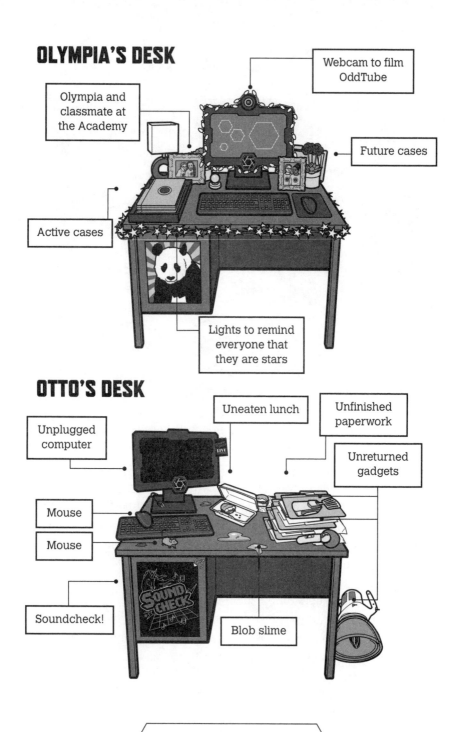

OLYMPIA'S DESK

Webcam to film OddTube

Olympia and classmate at the Academy

Future cases

Active cases

Lights to remind everyone that they are stars

OTTO'S DESK

Uneaten lunch

Unfinished paperwork

Unplugged computer

Unreturned gadgets

Mouse

Mouse

Soundcheck!

Blob slime

33 - 1 = 32

OLAF'S DESK

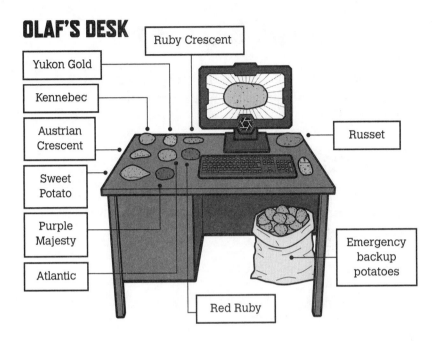

Ruby Crescent

Yukon Gold

Kennebec

Austrian Crescent

Sweet Potato

Purple Majesty

Atlantic

Russet

Emergency backup potatoes

Red Ruby

OTIS'S DESK

ENTER PASSWORD

11 + 11 + 11 = 33

THE BALL PIT

Want to get together with your fellow agents for a meeting? Use the ball pit. It's fun, colorful, and kind of smells like feet. But clean feet!

RESERVING THE BALL PIT FOR A MEETING

Since the ball pit is the only meeting room in your precinct, you must reserve it ahead of time. Here is the only Odd Squad–approved way to do that:

1. Run over to the ball pit as fast as you can.

2. Touch the side of the pit or a ball inside it.

3. Yell "Called it!"

4. If no one else touched the pit and yelled "Called it!" before you, it's all yours.

ARE YOU REALLY IN THE BALL PIT?

Unsure if you are inside the ball pit or not? Here is a flow chart to help you:

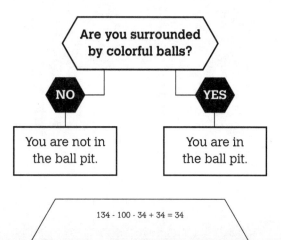

Are you surrounded by colorful balls?

NO → You are not in the ball pit.

YES → You are in the ball pit.

134 - 100 - 34 + 34 = 34

GETTING WHAT YOU NEED FROM THE BALL PIT

The ball pit can give you whatever you need. For example, say you don't have anything to write notes with. Not a problem. Just reach inside the pit with your hand. When you take your hand out, you will be holding a pen. Or the ball pit will give you a pencil with an eraser if the ball pit thinks you will make a mistake.

Many agents have asked how the ball pit is able to give you what you need. Is it magic? No. Here is exactly how it works:

$$0 = {}^{\psi}\phi^{H\vartheta\zeta Y} \times \pi + \boxed{\text{pie}} \times 6\Sigma/45 - \Psi^{\pi} \div \langle\!\!\!\rangle + \Delta^2 \times \pi\Phi_{\nu\partial\mu}$$

$$- (W^4 + \Delta x^5) \Diamond + \phi\chi\int\!\sqrt{} + \Omega\mu^{35} - \tfrac{1}{4} + (\!(X^{\delta} \times Y^2 \div \Omega)\!) +$$

$$f \div \overset{\text{deer}}{}{}_{81} - \tfrac{1}{49} \times \yen^{\wedge 8} \div (\textstyle\sum^{T} \times \sqrt{}) + \star\!\int\!\infty 6 - 1069 +$$

$$2\Delta + {}^{M}\Theta \div {}^{\psi}\phi^{H\vartheta\zeta Y}\pi + 45 - \circledcirc - \Psi^{\pi} + \Delta^2 \times \pi\Phi_{\nu\partial\mu} -$$

$$\circledcirc^2 - (W^4 + \Delta x^5) + \tfrac{1}{2} \div \phi\chi\int\!\sqrt{\%} + \blacktriangle\,\Omega\mu^{35} - \tfrac{1}{4} + \text{🔒}$$

$$(X^{\delta} \times Y^2 \div \Omega) \,\text{🐕}\, f\,{}_{81}\geq - \tfrac{1}{4} + \yen^3 \times \circledast (\textstyle\sum^{T} \times \sqrt{}) + \int\!\hbar - 10^{99}$$

$$+ 2\Delta \times y°F + 1 \times \circledcirc\; (\text{🔅} + c) \times ab + ac \times ab + \text{abracadabra}$$

$$(\!(ba \div x2 - -1 + (x\text{-}1) - (x\text{+}1)\!) + (F - 32) \div \vartheta\varkappa^{\vartheta\zeta Y}\pi\,\text{📷}$$

$$+ 45 - \epsilon^{\pi} + \Delta^7 \times \pi\varrho - (\Diamond^4 \times x^5) + \phi\chi\int\!\sqrt{} + \Omega\mu^{35} - \tfrac{3}{4} +$$

$$(X^{\delta} \times Y^2 \div \Omega)\, f\,{}_{81}\geq - \tfrac{1}{4} + \yen^3 \times (\textstyle\sum^{T} \times \sqrt{}) + \int\!\hbar - 10^{49} +$$

$$\text{🔒} \times 2\partial + 3^M \times Z\mathcal{E} + (b + c) \times xb + 10^{49} \times yb\,\boxed{\text{pie}}$$

$$(x^2 - \text{-}6^{\infty}) + (\Box - 32) \div Sn + y(\text{6}) \times \tfrac{1}{2}\,\infty + \theta\delta\pi^{\pi}$$

$$3\Delta + {}^{M}\Theta \div \varkappa^{H\vartheta\zeta Y}\pi + 49 - \circledcirc - \Omega\iota^{\pi} + \Delta^2 \times \odot\Delta -$$

$$- (\beta^{10} + x^{90210}) + \tfrac{1}{2} \div \phi\chi\int\!\sqrt{\%}\,v + \langle\!\!\!\rangle\,\Omega\mu^{35} - \tfrac{1}{4}$$

40 - 5 = 35

THE HALL OF DOORS

There are so many doors and hallways in Odd Squad headquarters, if we listed them all in this handbook, it would make the book bigger than the entire Earth. And since you're reading this book on Earth . . . well, let's just say that things would get really complicated really fast.

Instead of listing every door, here's a tip for how to figure out what is inside each one: Look at the decoration on the outside.

For example, if you're looking for the light bulb room, chances are there will be a bunch of light bulbs on the outside. Unless you just found the bright idea room. In that case, go inside and we bet you will get a bright idea where to find the light bulb room.

HERE ARE EXAMPLES OF OTHER DOORS AND WHAT YOU CAN FIND INSIDE:

THE PIANO ROOM

What's inside: So many pianos.

How you can tell: Big piano keys. Also, put your ear up to the door and you can usually hear Agent Ozart playing a beautiful symphony.

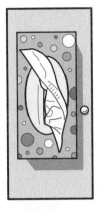

THE SICK GIANT ROOM

What's inside: Giants who have bad colds and need rest.

How you can tell: The giant tissue box. If you also bring some cough drops when you visit, the giants will love you for it.

THE TEDDY BEAR ROOM

What's inside: Teddy bears.

How you can tell: All the teddy bears. This one is pretty self-explanatory.

THE INVISIBLE ROOM

What's inside: An entire invisible city.

How you can tell: Lucky guess.

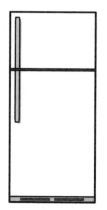

THE FINE ART ROOM

What's inside: Beautiful works of art made by Odd Squad staff.

How you can tell: It's a refrigerator door, and kids often hang their art on refrigerators with magnets. Odd Squad is proud of how super clever this one is.

THE TAKE-A-BUS-TO-YOUR-AUNT-JANE'S-HOUSE ROOM

What's inside: A bus that can take you to your Aunt Jane's house if you have an Aunt Jane.

How you can tell: The door is shaped like a rectangle, and a bus is kind of shaped like a rectangle. The knob is a circle, which, according to studies, is the favorite shape of nine out of ten Aunt Janes.*

Also, if you look closely, you'll see the name of the room written in tiny letters at the top of the door.

THE SECRET ROOM

What's inside: We can't tell you that.

How you can tell: Oh no, you already know too much.

THE BREAK ROOM

This is where agents can go if they want a break. We will leave the rest of this page blank in case you need a break from this handbook.

13 + 13 + 13 = 39

THE LABORATORY

The laboratory is where all the scientists work. It is filled with gadgets and other machines to help Odd Squad stop oddness. It used to be a flower shop and so people still stop by every once in a while on Valentine's Day or Mother's Day or if their friend is performing on stage and they want to give them something nice afterward to say, "Hey, good job, you!" If that happens, the scientists are more than happy to use the flower-inator to help them out.

As an agent, there are four reasons you will find yourself in the lab:

○ You are checking out a gadget.

○ You are returning a gadget.

○ It's a good shortcut to the cafeteria.

○ You are friends with a scientist and the scientist always goes to your desk to visit and so it's only fair that you go to where they are to keep things fairsies.

Orchid's favorite number = 40

YOUR UNIFORM & OTHER THINGS YOU WEAR

As an Odd Squad agent, you are expected to wear a uniform at all times, and it includes your badge, watch, and sneakers. You can take your sneakers off if you're at the beach because it's fun to feel your toes in the sand. You can also leave them on if the sand is really hot.

You should have received your uniform when you graduated from Odd Squad Academy. Remember that medium-size pineapple Professor O handed you along with your diploma? There's a uniform hidden inside. We'll wait while you open it up and check.

See? Told you. Why does Odd Squad hide uniforms inside pineapples? Fantastic question. We hope you enjoy the rest of segment five!

41 + 41 - 41 = 41

A GUIDE TO YOUR UNIFORM

BY AGENTs OLIVE and Otto

Greetings. My name is Agent Olive. As a professional agent who has worked at Odd Squad for several years, I have been tasked with writing this introduction about your agent uniform.

Actually, my partner, Otto, was supposed to write this with me, but he never turned in his sections. I'm not really sure what happened. Regardless, I will continue on because, as stated earlier, I am a professional.

Hi! Otto here! Sorry. I was stuck dealing with these creatures called Centigurps. Whoo! Those things are trouble. But...good news! I went to the Odd Squad Printing Press and Agent Omorro said it's too late to add pages, but I can write in the margins like this. Thanks, Omorro!

At Odd Squad, everyone is equal and everyone belongs. That is one reason why all agents wear the same uniform. Another reason is so anyone with an odd problem can immediately recognize an agent and ask for help. One time somebody thought I was a tiny businessperson because of my suit, and I got to go to an office building and make lots of big decisions. That business isn't around anymore now.☹ A third reason is because if agents didn't wear uniforms they would get cold or sunburned, depending on the weather.

This segment includes instructions for how to use the most current agent uniform, model #B7456H89876. If you have model #B7456H89874, that's okay. These instructions still work, but just do them all backward. Your uniform includes a shirt, pants, jacket, shoes, socks, belt, badge, and watch.

Remember, while wearing your uniform you are representing Odd Squad and all that it stands for. You have big shoulder pads to fill, but I know you can do it. ⟵——————— Awwww. Olive always says nice stuff like that.

By my calculations, the text has filled the allotted space and this introduction is now over. ⟵——— Wow, she's good.

Good luck, agents. We're all counting on you.

↖ ⎰ I think she said that because we do a lot of math. Also, bye!

Todd's page = 43

ARE YOU WEARING YOUR UNIFORM CORRECTLY?

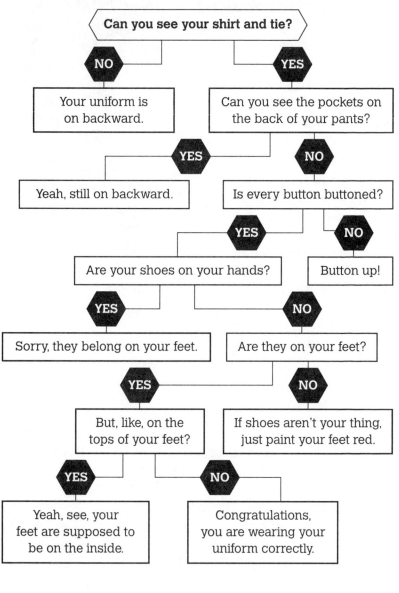

Can you see your shirt and tie?

NO → Your uniform is on backward.

YES → Can you see the pockets on the back of your pants?

YES → Yeah, still on backward.

NO → Is every button buttoned?

NO → Button up!

YES → Are your shoes on your hands?

YES → Sorry, they belong on your feet.

NO → Are they on your feet?

NO → If shoes aren't your thing, just paint your feet red.

YES → But, like, on the tops of your feet?

YES → Yeah, see, your feet are supposed to be on the inside.

NO → Congratulations, you are wearing your uniform correctly.

11 + 11 + 11 + 11 = 44

SECRET SUIT FUNCTIONS

Your suit has hundreds of secret functions, which you can learn about from your local Odd Squad tailor, O'Que. If you don't know who your O'Que is, look for the best-dressed kid in the office.

If you can't find O'Que, here are some secret functions while you are looking:

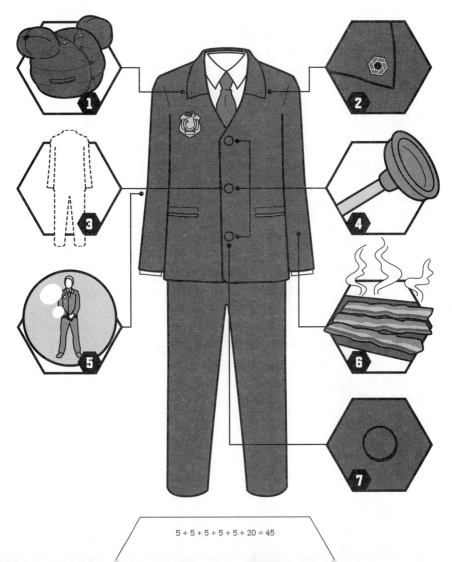

5 + 5 + 5 + 5 + 5 + 20 = 45

OFFICIAL UNIFORM FUNCTIONS

 Water Travel: Pull the yellow tabs under your collar to prepare for water travel.

 Homing Beacon: Tap the agent pins to activate your homing beacon so other agents can find you.

 Camouflage: Tap the middle button on your coat to blend in to your surroundings.

 Plunger Power: Tap all your buttons at once to blast a plunger across the room. This comes in handy if there is something across the room that you can't reach or if there is a friend across the room who needs a plunger.

 Force Field: Tap your elbows together 90 million times to create an impenetrable force field for 1 second.

 Griddle Activation: Raise your left arm to chest level and bend inward to activate a stove on your sleeve.

 Button: This one is just a button.

HOW TO TIE YOUR TIE

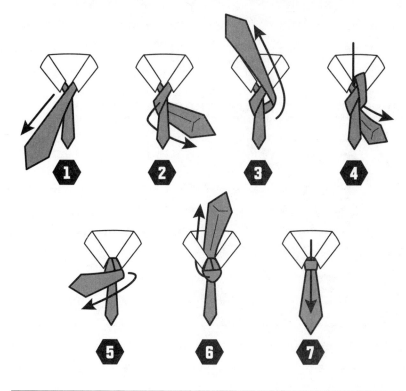

1 Cross the wide end over the small end.

2 Tuck the wide end under the small end.

3 Pull the wide end up and over, crossing the small end.

4 Pull the wide end through the loop.

5 Cross the wide end back over the small end.

6 Put the wide end through the loop.

7 Pull the wide end through the knot and tighten.

40 + 7 = 47

REPLACEMENT UNIFORMS

Accidents happen on the job. One of those accidents may involve your suit getting destroyed. If that happens, not to worry. You can regrow a new suit and badge within minutes.

HERE ARE STEP-BY-STEP INSTRUCTIONS

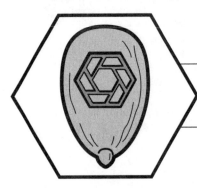

STEP 1: Go to your local lab and request an agent suit seed.

STEP 2: Fill a bucket with one gallon of water. If you do not have a one-gallon container, here are other ways to make a gallon.

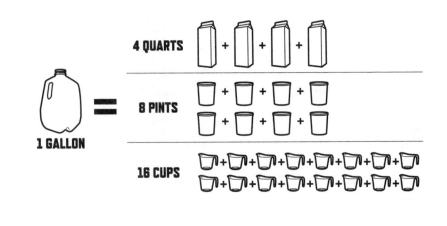

STEP 3: Drop the agent suit seed into the water.

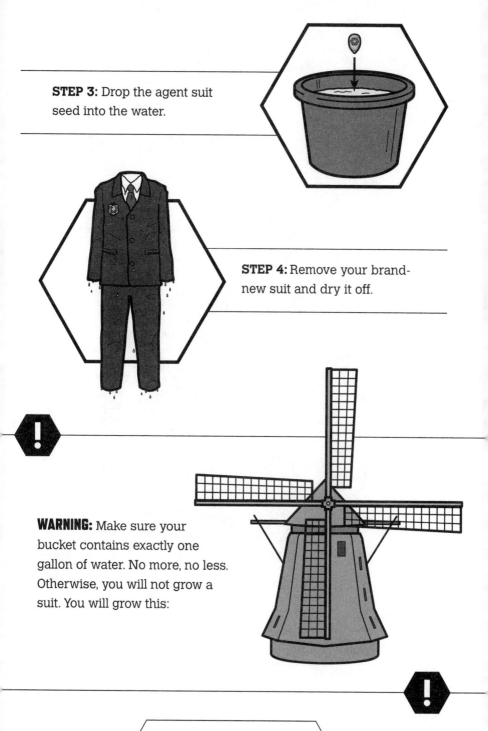

STEP 4: Remove your brand-new suit and dry it off.

WARNING: Make sure your bucket contains exactly one gallon of water. No more, no less. Otherwise, you will not grow a suit. You will grow this:

50 - 1 = 49

REASONS FOR REPLACEMENT UNIFORMS

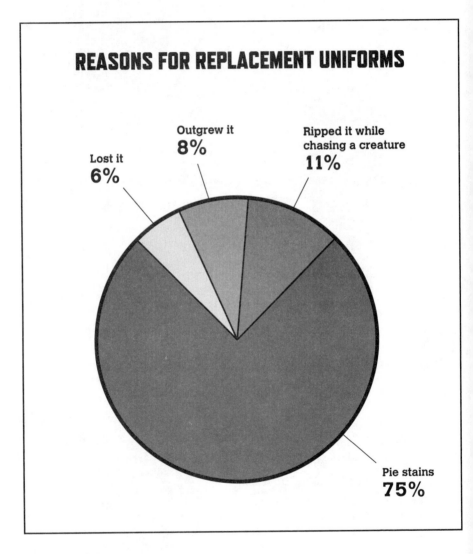

Outgrew it
8%

Lost it
6%

Ripped it while
chasing a creature
11%

Pie stains
75%

0 + 0 + 0 + 0 + 0 + 50 = 50

YOUR BADGE NUMBER

Your suit comes with a badge. On your badge is your agent number. But what happens when an angry badger uses its tiny badger teeth to gnaw on your badge until you can't read the number anymore?

Not to worry. It's easy to find your agent number again, with the help of this handy-dandy wheel:

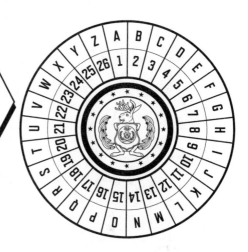

STEP 1: Use the wheel to find the numbers that go with the letters in your name. For example, if your name is OSCAR, the numbers that go with your name are:

O = 15   S = 19   C = 3   A = 1   R = 18

STEP 2: Add up the numbers. In the case of Oscar, his badge number is:

15 + 19 + 3 + 1 + 18 = 56

STEP 3: Use a marker or pen to write your number on the gnawed-off part on your badge. Show the badger you fixed it, and prove that badger is not the boss of you.

0 + 0 + 0 + 0 + 0 + 50 + 1 = 51

HOW TO USE YOUR BADGE PHONE

YOUR BADGE IS ALSO A PHONE

The phone opens like this:

If you open it the other way, it will look like this:

26 + 26 = 52

1. HOW TO ANSWER YOUR PHONE

As an Odd Squad agent, you may answer your phone however you like. Here are some examples:

Good morning, sunshine.

Ornando's House of Pizza! Ask us about our garlic knots.

Sorry. Wrong number.

Hi. Hi. Hi. Hi.

[*We don't suggest you use this greeting, as it is confusing.*]

fiffy thwee + spell-check = 53

2. SET YOUR RINGTONE

Badge phones come with the Odd Squad theme as the ringtone. But you can also change it. If you're feeling dance-y, try Soundcheck's "Up Down Left Right." If you are undercover on an important case or at the movies, please turn your ringtone off.

3. DON'T GO OVER YOUR MINUTES LIMIT

Each agent is allotted 43,100 minutes of phone use per month. Going over this limit will cause your phone to be turned into a medium-size dalmatian.

4. HOW TO MAKE INTERNATIONAL CALLS

Say "Make a call, please" in the language of the country you wish to call, while eating food from that country and quietly whispering the name of its most popular sport. Or dial 9.

HELPFUL SPEED DIAL CODES

#0	Your Ms. or Mr. O's office
#00	The Big O's office
#1	You
#2	Your partner
#12	You and your partner at the same time
#747	Your partner if your partner is on a plane
#317537	Sheila (She won't be able to see you, but hopefully she can hear you.)

5 with a 4 after = 54

COMMON BADGE PHONE FUNCTIONS

> Tap phone twice: Set an alarm.

> Swipe phone left: Play music.

> Swipe phone right: Turn off music.

> Spin phone on table: Create a soft breeze.

> Gently shake phone up and down: Produce salt and pepper.

LESS COMMON BADGE PHONE FUNCTIONS

> Lounge chair for a bug.

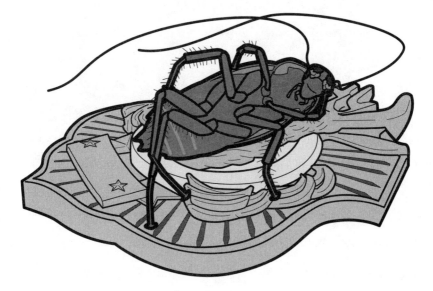

11 + 11 + 11 + 11 + 11 = 55

HOW TO USE YOUR WATCH TABLET

The most common way to use your watch tablet is to tap the watch twice with two fingers, and then the watch tablet screen will become a large hexagon. A hexagon is a six-sided shape. It looks like this:

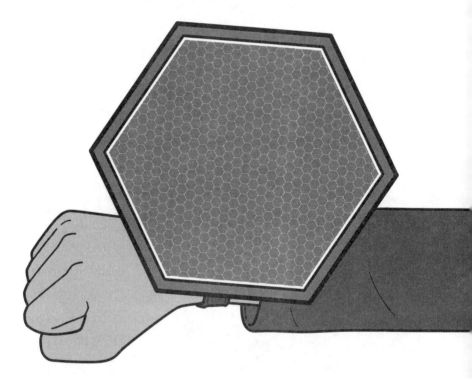

But did you know you can make your watch tablet into other shapes, too? If your answer is "yes" you can turn the page now. If you answered "no," here are some other shapes you can try, with instructions on how to make them.

50 + 6 = 56

A flower: Tap twice with your thumb, then swipe.

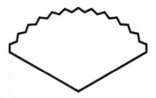

A fan: Flick your wrist quickly.

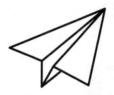

A paper airplane: Tap once and shake twice.

An origami swan: Tap once and trace the shape of a swan.

The state of Georgia: Tap twice with two fingers while eating a peach.

A vase: Tap all five knuckles, but delicately.

Two people talking: See instructions for vase.

Next page - 1 = 57

GADGETS

Howdy do, agents! Oona here to talk about my favorite topic: overalls. Why are they called overalls? They don't go over your arms or your head. I think they should be called overmosts. You know what I mean?

Now let's talk about my second favorite topic: gadgets. As an Odd Squad lab director, I get to build and fix so many incredible gadgets that can do so many incredible things. And gadgets are used to fix any odd problem in the world, right?

Wrong.

Huh?

Wrong.

No, I heard me the first time, I just don't understand.

Let me explain. Gadgets don't solve odd problems. Agents do. Gadgets are tools. Just like hammers or screwdrivers or that pointy thing the dentist uses to clean your teeth. Sure, gadgets are powerful. But they're not as powerful as hard work, or thinking a problem through, or trying again if you don't solve it the first time.

That's why I like to say that the best gadget is the one you always have with you: your brain-inator. Also known as your brain. Also known as your Think-er-Doodle, but only by my friend Shelly. She has such a fun way with words.

Bottom line: Think before blasting a gadget. Maybe you will discover the problem can be solved by talking things out with your partner. Or writing your thoughts out with a pencil. Or talking things out with a talking pencil. Um, actually, if you see a talking pencil please use the Un-talk-inator gadget right away. I've chatted with a few pencils, and things can get awkward fast.

All righty. I hope you find the rest of this gadget guide helpful. I'm not sure how to end this. How about with a karate kick?

Yow!

Yeah, that felt pretty good.

58 + 2 + 8 - 9 = 59

THE ALMOST IMPOSSIBLE-TO-USE GADGET

Most gadgets are very simple to use. Let's say you want to use the shrink-inator. You need to simply press the button, and—zap—it works. A very simple process. So simple that even a villain could do it. But there's one gadget few dare to try. It's called the clap-inator. Now if you think this sounds ridiculous, you're right. This should not be a complicated gadget. It is only used to make clapping sounds.

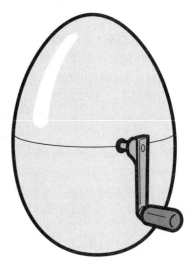

But there's so much to do to make it work. You will not find any buttons. It's shaped like an egg, with an odd crank. But do you think you crank it? No. You have to cackle at it. Like a villain. The ball will start shaking until the crank can turn by itself. It then bakes a cookie. Resist eating it! Throw it into the mouth of a dragon. The dragon will breathe fire. If you dare not run, you'll hear clapping. Take a bow.

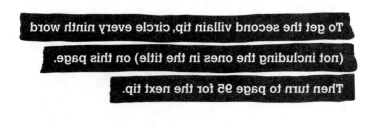

To get the second villain tip, circle every ninth word (not including the ones in the title) on this page.

Then turn to page 95 for the next tip.

20 + 20 + 20 = 60

MOST POPULAR GADGETS

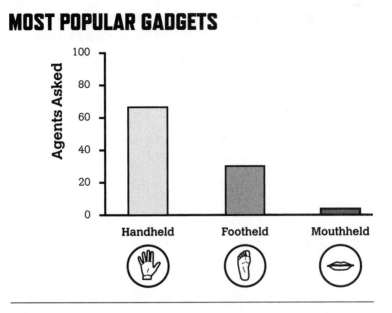

MOST POPULAR GADGET SOUNDS

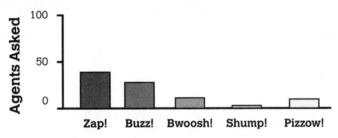

MOST POPULAR GADGET COLORS

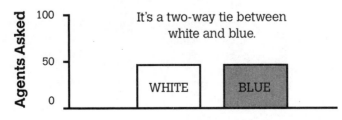

It's a two-way tie between white and blue.

62 - 1 = 61

GADGET SIGN-OUT SHEET

NAME	BADGE NUMBER	TIME	GADGET SIGNED OUT	WHY NEEDED
Olympia	91	7:59 A.M.	Invisible-inator	Villain stakeout
Otis	63	9:20 A.M.	Un-truck-inator	Truck
Orchid	57	10:30 A.M.	Un-pancake-inator	Giant evil pancakes
Ocean	38	Morning Or night	Fur-inator	Creature missing fur and is chilly

31 twice = 62

If you need a gadget from the lab, please remember to sign out the gadget before using it. Here is an example sign-out sheet from Precinct #13579, which was filled out on June 4, 2016

HOW IS YOUR DAY GOING?	HOW IS YOUR DAY GOING?	PLEASE DRAW A PICTURE FOR THE ENJOYMENT OF THE ODD SQUAD SCIENTISTS
Really great. First I woke up just before my alarm. I love when that happens because then I can get a jump on the day. Then my alarm went off, and it was playing a great song that I'd never heard before, and I remember thinking, "Huh, how could this song seem so familiar but unfamiliar at the same . . . (continued on pages 2 through 81)	I dreamed that I was traveling around the Earth, but it wasn't our Earth, but it looked just like our Earth. And also I don't think I was in my body, but it looked just like my body, actually it might have been my . . . (continued on pages 2 through 95)	
Fine.	N/A	——
No time to talk, Sherman.	I'll tell you later.	
Pretty good, dude. How is yours?	I was riding in a boat but in the sky. Also the boat looked like a plane.	This is what the dude will look like with fur.

21 + 21 + 21 = 63

NAME	BADGE NUMBER	TIME	GADGET SIGNED OUT	WHY NEEDED
Orchid	Still 57	1:30 P.M.	Un-blueberry-pancake-inator	Apparently there were blueberries in the giant evil pancakes.
Owen	Also 57. Huh, never noticed that.	1:45 P.M.	Pillow-inator	Going on break
Orchid	57. Owen should change his badge number! I was here first.	3:06 P.M.	Un-blueberry-whole-wheat-pancake-inator	How was I supposed to know they were whole wheat???
Ohlm	48	3:30 P.M.	Chaos-inator	To destroy Odd Squad
Orchid	57. Always 57.	4:30 P.M.	Bubble-bath-inator	After all that, the pancakes went away by themselves, so it was a huge waste of time and I REALLY need to relax.

46 reversed = 64

HOW IS YOUR DAY GOING?	WHAT DID YOU DREAM ABOUT LAST NIGHT?	PLEASE DRAW A PICTURE FOR THE ENJOYMENT OF THE ODD SQUAD SCIENTISTS
Same but a little more annoying	See above.	
A lot of work so far. I could use a break.	A break	Sorry, gotta run.
Getting iffier	I wish this was a dream.	
Does anybody actually read this thing? I didn't think so.	Total world domination	
Seriously?!	Stop asking me this question.	

5 + 15 + 25 + 15 + 5 = 65

A GUIDE TO COMMONLY USED GADGETS

SHRINK-INATOR

GADGET
8
NUMBER

FUNCTION: Shrinking things.

BEST USED FOR: Dealing with giant creatures.

ALTERNATIVE USE: Great for getting your partner through a keyhole.

CAUTION: Do not shrink your shrink-inator. It will be so small that you'll have to get the Ant Odd Squad involved, and then it's a whole thing.

PUDDING-INATOR

GADGET
65
NUMBER

FUNCTION: Turn anything into pudding.

BEST USED FOR: Distracting creatures that like pudding.

ALTERNATIVE USE: A quick and easy weeknight dessert.

CAUTION: Not available in butterscotch.

33 + 22 + 11 = 66

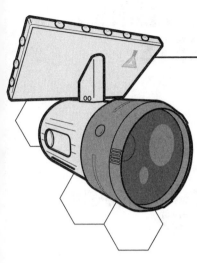

DAY-INATOR

FUNCTION: Time travel to any day of your choosing.

BEST USED FOR: Making today your birthday when you're in a party mood.

ALTERNATIVE USE: Making it Grilled Cheese Day at the cafeteria.

CAUTION: Beware the Time Sheep.

FLIP-FLOP-INATOR

GADGET
9
NUMBER

FUNCTION: Flips the places of digits in a two-digit number. Example: 12 flips to 21.

BEST USED FOR: Flipping the digits of your age.

ALTERNATIVE USE: Flipping the digits of a page number in a book.

CAUTION: Will not work on anybody who is 11. Or 22. Or 33. Or 44. (You can see where this is going.)

A GUIDE TO UNCOMMONLY USED GADGETS

MOVE-THAT-PEN-TO-THE-LEFT-INATOR

This gadget will move that pen a little bit to the left. Not just any pen, but that pen. It's kind of hard to explain without showing you in person.

NAME-A-FERRET-DANIEL-INATOR

This gadget can change the legal name of any ferret to Daniel. The ferret's name can be changed back either by using the Un-name-a-ferret-Daniel-inator or by filling out a lot of paperwork at City Hall.

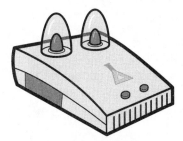

SEE-YOU-LATER-ALLIGATOR-INATOR

This gadget will say the phrase "see you later, alligator" if you want to say it but just can't muster up the energy to say it yourself.

SALT-SHAKER-INATOR

This cylindrical gadget has a series of "micro holes" on the top of the unit. For best use, grip the center of the device and rotate vertically until the micro holes are positioned over a food item. Tiny grains of salt will fall from the unit onto the food and improve the flavor.

NOTE: Agents must complete a mandatory four-week training course for this gadget.

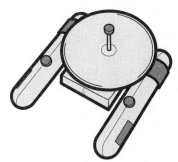

REASONABLY-PRICED-BEANS-INATOR

This will give any agent who uses it the powers of flight, infinite strength, and never-ending joy. This gadget might be more popular if it had a different name.

HOW TO COMBINE GADGETS

When you're out on a case, sometimes you won't have the gadget you're looking for. Not to worry. You can make a new gadget with the gadgets you have. Every gadget has a number on the bottom. So you just combine other gadgets so their numbers add up to the number of the one you need.

For example, let's say that you're being chased by a hungry Pie Dragon, but you don't have gadget number 12, the Apple-Pie-inator. Here are just some of the ways you can combine other gadgets to make number 12:

$7 + 5 = 12$ $\qquad$ $6 + 6 = 12$ $\qquad$ $11 + 1 = 12$

$8 + 4 = 12$ $\qquad$ $9 + 3 = 12$

But if you really want to impress your partner, you can combine more than two numbers to get the number you're looking for:

$2 + 2 + 2 + 2 + 2 + 2 = 12$

$2 + 2 + 2 + 2 + 2 + 1 + 1 = 12$

$1 + 1 + 1 + 1 + 1 + 1 + 1 + 1 + 1 + 1 + 1 + 1 = 12$

If you don't have any of the above combinations available, we recommend making your own pie from scratch. There is a recipe on page 72 you can use. Oh, and we suggest asking a grown-up to help. You know, just to make them feel useful.

$50 + 15 + 5 = 70$

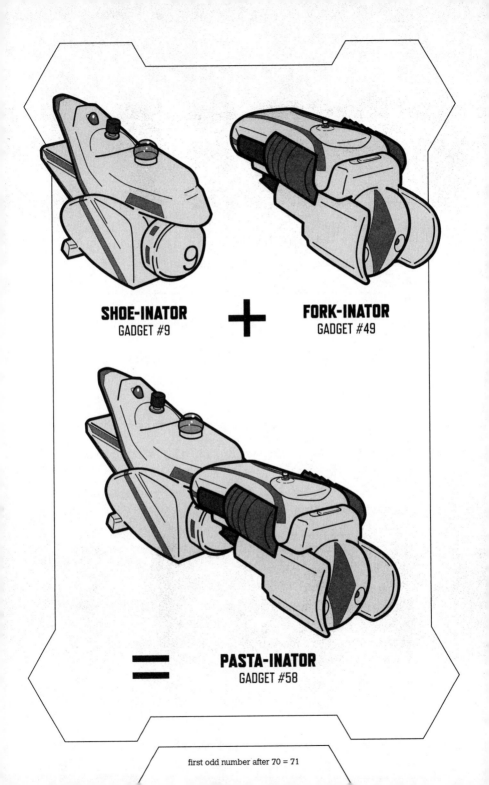

SHOE-INATOR
GADGET #9

+

FORK-INATOR
GADGET #49

=

PASTA-INATOR
GADGET #58

first odd number after 70 = 71

ODD SQUAD
APPLE PIE RECIPE

MAKE THE PIECRUST

Makes two piecrusts (one for the top and one for the bottom)

2½ cups sifted flour	16 tablespoons cold butter
2 tablespoons sugar	8 tablespoons vegetable shortening
2 teaspoons salt	½ to 1 cup cold water

1) Mix dry ingredients and place them in a large food processor or a large bowl.

2) Chop cold butter into cubes.

3) Add cold butter and vegetable shortening to food processor or bowl.

4) Pulse in food processor or mix in bowl until yellow and mealy.

5) Take mixture out of food processor and put in bowl. Add cold water and mix with a fork.

36 + 36 = 72

6) Form into two fist-size balls of dough. Each of these balls will be one crust. Cover ball with light coating of flour so it sticks together. NOTE: If it is too wet and hard to handle, feel free to add more flour.

7) Move each ball of dough onto a flat surface and flatten into a small disc. Wrap each flattened disc of dough in plastic wrap or wax paper and place in refrigerator for at least one hour. You can also freeze the dough if you want to finish making the pie later.

MAKE THE FILLING

Makes filling for one deep-dish pie.

8 apples (We like Pink Lady or Jonagold, but any kind will do.)

1 cup white sugar

½ cup brown sugar

1 teaspoon cinnamon

Healthy sprinkle of cloves

Healthy sprinkle of nutmeg

5 tablespoons thickener (We like Clear Jel but cornstarch will also work.)

1) Peel and thinly slice apples. Add to a bowl.

2) Combine dry ingredients except thickener.

3) Mix apples and dry ingredients.

4) Mix in thickener.

PUT IT ALL TOGETHER

You will need an additional 2–3 tablespoons of butter and an egg for this step.

1) Take cold pie discs of dough out of the refrigerator and roll flat.

2) Fold the dough back together into a small square. (This creates layers of butter, which will expand and cause flakiness.)

3) Roll the dough out again into a wide circle.

4) Place dough in the bottom of your pie dish (metal recommended).

5) Dump the pie filling into the crust.

6) Dot the top of the filling with 2–3 tablespoons of butter.

7) Cover with second piecrust dough.

8) Trim the edges of the piecrust so only 1–2 inches are hanging over the edge of the pie dish. Then use a fork or your fingers to press the two crusts together and seal everything in.

$$4 + 70 + 70 - 70 + 70 - 70 = 74$$

9) Cut 2–3 small holes in the top of the crust so hot air can escape.

10) Beat a whole egg in a small bowl.

11) Use a pastry brush to cover the top crust with egg for a shiny finish. You can also lightly sprinkle the top of the pie with sugar, or sugar and cinnamon for a crunchier texture.

BAKING

1) Place on a cookie sheet (in case it drips).

2) Bake 20 minutes on 450 degrees.

3) Remove and put aluminum foil around edges to protect the crust from burning. You can also use a metal piecrust protector.

4) Lower oven to 350 degrees. Cook for 60 more minutes.

EATING

1) Use a pie or cake slicer to cut triangle-shaped pieces for you and your friends and loved ones.

2) Put vanilla ice cream on top, if you want.

3) Eat your pie.

4) Enjoy this wonderful moment.

25 + 25 + 25 = 75

YOUR PARTNER

OLYMPIA: Gah! Wow. When we were asked to write something for the new edition of the *Odd Squad Agent's Handbook*, I kind of flipped out. At the academy I used to read my copy of the handbook over and over, and I knew the entire thirty-seventh edition by heart. So this is exciting. Aren't you excited, Otis?

OTIS: I am.

OLYMPIA: That's my partner, Otis. He's a pretty amazing guy.

OTIS: Thanks.

38 + 38 - 38 + 38 = 76

OLYMPIA: Partnership is so important at Odd Squad. Without a partner, you would just be talking to yourself a lot. Or you would go into Ms. O's office and she'd say, *There you one are.* Which is both weird and bad grammar. Right, Otis?

OTIS: Yes.

OLYMPIA: See what I mean? It's sooo helpful to have somebody like Otis to talk to. When we started out we didn't even know each other. And now we practically share a brain. Otis, what am I thinking about right now?

OTIS: This book.

OLYMPIA: Well, I was thinking about pandas, but we can't be all right all the time. But if you make a mistake, your partner is there to catch it. So you don't need to have all the answers, because there are two of you. Well, unless you just got zapped by a Double-inator. Then there would be four of you.

OTIS: Ha.

OLYMPIA: Otis also gets my jokes! That's another thing, you can't be so serious all the time. You have to have some fun.

OTIS: I enjoy fun.

seven + "T" + "seven" = 77

OLYMPIA: But don't worry if you and your new partner aren't best buds from the beginning. It can take time. There are a bunch of helpful tips in this handbook for you to get to know each other better and make your partnership as strong as it can be. Otis, do you have anything else to say?

OTIS: No.

OLYMPIA: Okay, well, we wish you and your partner much—

OTIS: Wait. I do have something to say.

OLYMPIA: It's kind of weird how you interrupted me in a book.

OTIS: I know. Anyway, I want to say that your partner is not just somebody you work with. Your partner is also a friend. Somebody who knows you better than anybody else. Somebody who supports you when times are tough and challenges you to be a better agent, and a better person, than you ever thought you could be.

OLYMPIA: Wait a minute, Otis. Are you saying that about me?

OTIS: . . .

OLYMPIA: Aww. That guy.

GET TO KNOW YOUR PARTNER

Chances are you will be meeting your partner for the first time when you arrive at your new headquarters. Here are some ways you can get to know your partner quickly.

USE A CONVERSATION STARTER

> "If you were an odd creature, what odd creature would you be?"

> "I like your tie. It looks similar to mine!"

> "I noticed your name also starts with *O*. Small world!"

> "If you could be any ice cream flavor in the world . . . Well, that would be weird, because you are a human being, not ice cream."

TRY A GETTING-TO-KNOW-YOU SONG

Get some pencils and paper. Write down everything you know about yourself, and your partner will do the same. Purchase or borrow two banjos. Find a banjo teacher and take a lesson. Tune your banjos. Then strum a little tune and sing your lists to each other. If you are moved to square dance, do so.

TAKE A FIELD TRIP

The best place to take a field trip with your new partner is to an empty field. There won't be much to do in the field, so it will force you to get to know each other. If you don't know what to talk about, talk about that time you went to an empty field together.

COMPLIMENT YOUR PARTNER

If your partner is wearing a hat, comment on the hat by saying, "Hey, nice hat." Say that you like the color: "Hey, is that blue? That looks blue to me. I like that shade of blue." If you really like the hat, ask to borrow it for the weekend. Or maybe a month. Or a year. Or ten years. Or forever and ever. If your partner says no, tell them how much you like their shoes and repeat the whole process.

SAVE YOUR TOWN FROM ODDNESS

There's no better way to get to know someone than working on an exciting project together. And what's more exciting than saving your town from an odd creature or villain? It'll force you to make a plan together, think together, run fast together, and say, "Odd Squad, stop right there!" together. Then you can talk about that time you saved the town together, and how it was better than the time you went to an empty field or argued about a hat.

DRAW A PICTURE TOGETHER

Draw a picture together. Here, we'll even start it for you.

20 + 20 + 20 + 20 = 80

WHEN NOTHING ODD IS HAPPENING

Waiting for something odd to happen? Here are suggestions for how you and your partner can spend your free time:

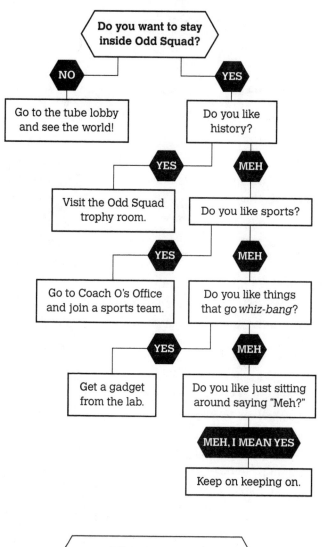

Do you want to stay inside Odd Squad?

NO → Go to the tube lobby and see the world!

YES → Do you like history?

YES → Visit the Odd Squad trophy room.

MEH → Do you like sports?

YES → Go to Coach O's Office and join a sports team.

MEH → Do you like things that go *whiz-bang*?

YES → Get a gadget from the lab.

MEH → Do you like just sitting around saying "Meh?"

MEH, I MEAN YES → Keep on keeping on.

Add nine 9s together = 81

ODD CREATURES

What's goin' on, agent dudes? My name's Ocean. Like the ocean. If you've never seen the ocean before, here's a drawing for you:

I run the creature room at Odd Squad Precinct #13579. One question I get asked a lot is: What's the difference between an animal and a creature?

That's important to know, because if an animal is lost or in trouble or causing trouble, it's not your job. It's more like a zookeeper/veterinarian/animal rescue type situation. I mean, hey, if you've got free time, definitely help those dudes out. But you're not the main dude in charge.

20 + 20 + 20 + 20 + 2 = 82

But if it's a creature that's lost or in trouble or causing trouble, that's all you, dude. And your partner. Hey, partner dude! Sorry, I didn't see you there.

Here's a checklist you can use to figure out if something is an animal or a creature:

C	**Creature-y.** Is the thing you're looking at kind of creature-y? If so, it's probably a creature.
R	**Run.** Does it make you want to run for your life? If so, definitely a creature.
E	**Eukaryotic organism.** If the dude you're looking at is that, it's probably an animal. Leave that dude alone.
A	**Arithmetic.** That's a fancy word for math. Creatures love to do math. If you see something furry adding or subtracting, that furry dude is probably a creature.
T	**Talk.** Most creatures talk! So just ask if it's a creature or not.
U	**Underwear.** Creatures always wear underwear. It might be hard to see because they have lots of fur or a protective outer skin situation. But if you catch a glimpse of underwear, you've got yourself a creature.
R	**Run.** If you are still running for your life, yeah, that's definitely a creature chasing you. Those dudes never get tired.
E	**Examine the chart.** If the other letters didn't help you out, check out the chart on the next page.

put an 8 next to a 3 = 83

CLASSIFICATION OF CREATURES

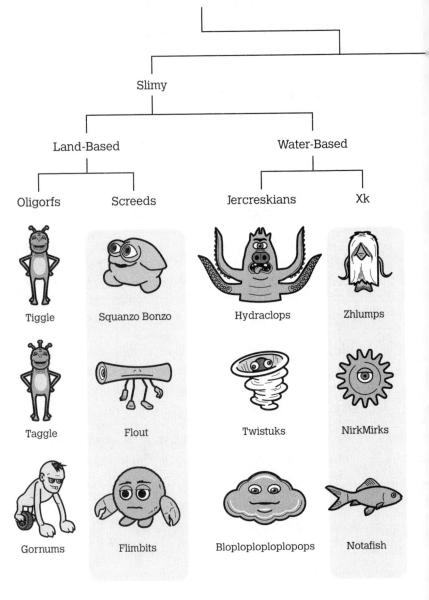

Slimy

Land-Based

Oligorfs

Tiggle

Taggle

Gornums

Screeds

Squanzo Bonzo

Flout

Flimbits

Water-Based

Jercreskians

Hydraclops

Twistuks

Bloploploploplopops

Xk

Zhlumps

NirkMirks

Notafish

7 + 70 + 7 = 84

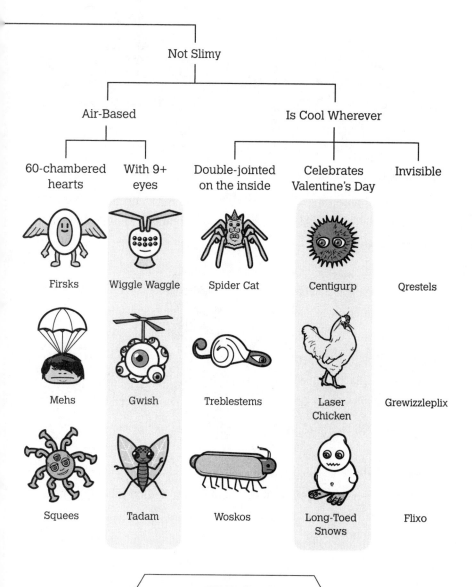

Not Slimy

Air-Based

60-chambered hearts

Firsks

Mehs

Squees

With 9+ eyes

Wiggle Waggle

Gwish

Tadam

Is Cool Wherever

Double-jointed on the inside

Spider Cat

Treblestems

Woskos

Celebrates Valentine's Day

Centigurp

Laser Chicken

Long-Toed Snows

Invisible

Qrestels

Grewizzleplix

Flixo

LXXXV = 85

WHAT TO DO IF YOU ARE SLIMED BY A BLOB

1. RUN

The best way to deal with a blob sliming is not to be slimed by a blob in the first place. If you see a blob, run the other way as fast as you can.

2. TALK

If the blob catches you, first try talking to it. You might try saying, "I wish you wouldn't attack me," or "What was it like growing up in Blobsylvania?"

3. WRESTLE

If running and talking don't work, you must wrestle the blob to the ground. This is difficult because blobs can split apart, and wrestling two blobs is harder than wrestling one blob. Wrestling nineteen blobs is almost impossible. On the plus side, it's hilarious to watch.

4. CONTAIN

Once you have pinned down the blob, put it in a container like a cup or a box. Be sure to cover the container. If you don't have a cover, repeat steps one through four for the rest of your life, or until somebody else comes to help.

22 + 22 + 22 + 22 - 1 = 87

HOW TO INTERROGATE A UNICORN

Unicorns are graceful and beautiful creatures. The first Odd Squad agent ever to see a unicorn was so inspired that he immediately wrote a poem. It went like this:

> *Look at that unicorn*
> *Run down that street.*
> *Wow. Wow. WOW!*

It wasn't a great poem. The agent was probably too overwhelmed by the unicorn's majestic beauty to come up with a good rhyme.

But don't be fooled. Yes, unicorns can be magnificent. But they're also sneaky and like to cause oddness. So sometimes you will have to interrogate them. "Interrogate" is a fancy word that means ask questions. Fancy words are helpful because they will make the unicorn think you are smart.

$$11 + 11 + 11 + 11 + 11 + 11 + 11 + 11 = 88$$

HERE IS A STEP-BY-STEP GUIDE:

1. MAKE THE UNICORN COMFORTABLE

Try playing some gentle harp music and offer the unicorn a snack. Most unicorns enjoy boiled hay with rainbow sprinkles.

2. TRICK THE UNICORN

Try holding up a mirror and saying "Who did it?" and see if the unicorn points at its reflection. **NOTE:** This doesn't always work, because many unicorns know this trick. **ANOTHER NOTE:** Please keep this handbook away from unicorns, because we don't want more of them to learn this trick.

3. MAKE THE UNICORN JEALOUS

If the unicorn still won't cooperate, then say, "Okay, I'll just have to talk to a Pegasus instead."

4. GO ON A MAGICAL JOURNEY

If you still haven't found out the truth, ask the unicorn to take you through a magical land of rainbows and clouds. The unicorn will always say yes to this. While on the trip, ask, "Hey, did ya do it? C'mon, did ya?" The unicorn will tell you the truth because it will be feeling so happy and free.

ODD DISEASES

My name is Dr. O. I am a doctor in Precinct #13579. You can tell I'm a doctor because I just said so and I have only told one lie in my life. That was the lie right there in the sentence before this.

An odd disease is a disease that is odd. Anyone can catch one including you.

Anybody can get an odd disease. Even a doctor. I am a doctor, and I have an odd disease that causes me to yell whenever I type words. Wow. The kid in the office next to me is not pleased right now.

30 + 30 + 30 = 90

Agents should check themselves every second on the second to make sure they don't have any odd diseases. If you find you do have one, visit the Dr. O in your Odd Squad immediately. If I am the doctor in your Odd Squad visit me. Hopefully I will be typing, then you can just walk toward the sound of yelling.

The following is a list of the most common odd diseases so you can do that checking thing I was just writing about.

What's next?

Oh yes, check out that list.

Yours in medicine,

Dr. O

LIST OF COMMON ODD DISEASES

1. Stripe-osis
2. Elf Rash
3. Cell Phone Tooth
4. Robot-theria
5. Everything-But-the-Kitchen-Sink Disease
6. The Jinx
7. Laughing Knuckle
8. You-Think-Every-Day-Is-Friday-itis
9. B-7 (aka the Bingo Disease)
10. Unicorn Sneeze
11. Icecuberculosis
12. Laughing Sallies
13. Dry Finger
14. Acronym D.I.S.E.A.S.E.
15. No-Way-Out Influenza
16. Oh-My-Body-Is Made-of-Clouds-Now-osis
17. The Sillies
18. Head Loss
19. Expensive Wrist Syndrome
20. Restless Moose Disease
21. Esaesid Drawkcab
22. Anti-anti-virus
23. Rubber Ball-theria
24. The Sing-alongs
25. Hickory Dickory Docks Disease
26. ALL CAPS FLU
27. Narwal Knees
28. Danthemandruff
29. The Up and Aways
30. Rooster Tongue
31. Inky Neck
32. Cosmic Snail Flu
33. Kitchen Sink Disease
34. The Common Carpet
35. Hurry Up and Waits

An easy one: 92 = 92

36. Excessive Waving Syndrome

37. Volcanus in Your Nose Eruptus

38. It's-Me-Not-You Pneumonia

39. Lemon Lips

40. Lime Lips

41. Aunt Lydia Deficiency

42. I-in-Team Cough

43. Ninja-tosis

44. Ice Cream Face

45. Not-February-Ever Disease

46. The Over and Outs

47. On-My-Way-to-San-Franciscosis

48. Chowder Thumb

49. Angry Sock Syndrome

50. Unicorn-emia

51. Snooze Button Affliction

52. It's-You-Not-Me Pneumonia

53. North Pacific Giggles

54. Grandpa's Folly

55. Outer Space Infection

56. Delaware Bird Cough

57. Doe's Toe

58. Never Say Never Runny Nose

59. Eyebrows Everywhere Disease

60. Slight Candlestick Affiliation

61. Severeness Everywhere

62. The See-Through-Yous

63. Hawaiian Sphinx Flu

64. Eyebrows Nowhere Disease

65. Resistance-Is-Futile Pox

66. Especiallies

67. Float-itis

68. Plaid-tosis

69. Pirate-itis

70. The Repeats

71. The Repeats

72. The Patty Cake, Patty Cakes

73. Polka-dot-itis

74. Cantaloupe Nails

31 + 31 + 31 = 93

75. Frog Lung

76. Whooping Bear Claw

77. Cat Nose

78. Monkey's Uncle

79. The Hop, Skip, and a-Jumps

80. The Upsie-Daisies

81. The Under-Doobsies

82. The No-I-Haven't-Seen-Michael-But-If-I-See-Him-I'll-Tell-Him-You-Were-Looking-for-Him-itis

83. Frying Pan Hand

84. Butter Brain

85. Butter Substitute Brain

86. The Michael-Someone-Was-Looking-for-Yous

87. The Paperfoot Diseases

88. The Creaks

89. Yogurt Teeth

90. The Scoops

91. The Double Scoops

92. The Double Scoops with Waffle Cone Variation

93. Starry, Starry Cough

94. Too-Much-Woodchuck-edola

95. Thigh Cloud

96. The Flibbity Jibbits

97. The Zooms

98. Pulled Mussel

99. Slippery Sock Syndrome

100. The Natural Aging Process Except 3 Percent Slower

101. Gasser's Drapery

102. The Happies

103. The What The's

104. The Cat's Meow

105. Twice as Long Arms as Usuals

106. Orthodontist's Upper Ear Infection

107. The Yip Yip Yip Yip Yips

108. Peanut Butter Legs

109. Twelve Finger Discomfort

110. Melon Blindness

111. Too Much Mazzy Starrinitis

112. Postnasal Sip

113. Hansel and Gretel–itis

114. Yzema
115. Stopwatch Syndrome
116. Mehydration
117. Muscle Lamps
118. Severeness Everywhere
119. Pulled Funny Bone
120. Moses-Supposes-His-Toeses-Are-Roses-itosis
121. Multiple Body Syndrome
122. The Hippity Hops
123. The Bippity Bops
124. The Shmippity Wippity Dippity Dops
125. I-Spy-Fluenza
126. The Weasel Measles
127. Clownitosis
128. Bouncing Brother Syndrome
129. Severe Yak's Breath
130. The Cutsie Wutsies
131. Tiny Magazine-itis
132. Soap Neck
133. Sudden Wing Syndrome
134. The Moth Condition

135. Walrus Fever
136. Dentist's Elbow
137. Pegasus Sweats
138. Borrowed Koala Disease
139. Bread Crust Chin
140. Laser Chicken Pox
141. Liquid Ankle
142. Pillowmania
143. Soup Plague
144. Hawaiian Sphinx Flu
145. Pizza Shins
146. The Hullabaloos
147. The Wa-Cha-Cha-Chas
148. The Giddyups
149. One-More-to-Go-ola
150. Slime Eye

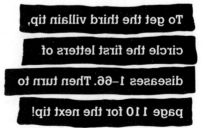

To get the third villain tip, circle the first letters of diseases 1–66. Then turn to page 110 for the next tip!

50 - 5 + 50 = 95

ODD VILLAINS & FLOATING SANDWICHES

Sorry, we don't have any tips for how to battle villains. There are definitely not any hidden anywhere inside this handbook, so if a villain finds this, that villain can just put the handbook down right now. Thank you.

54 + 32 + 10 = 96

FLOATING SANDWICHES

A floating sandwich is a sandwich that makes you float. It can happen to a person like this:

Or an animal, like this:

96's big brother by one year = 97

A floating sandwich can also make a regular nonfloating sandwich float like this:

Some in Odd Squad believe a floating sandwich has tiny creatures inside it that makes it float. Therefore, it should be considered an odd creature.

Others in Odd Squad believe a floating sandwich is a rare virus, which would make it an odd disease.

Still others in Odd Squad believe a floating sandwich has a personality and can talk, but it chooses not to. That would make it an odd villain.

Whichever category floating sandwiches do or do not fall into, we suggest you play it safe and eat a soup or salad instead.

WHEN SOMETHING VERY ODD HAS HAPPENED

At Odd Squad we have a very old saying: *Non opus est tibi ut opus est Latine discere hic.* It means, "You do not need to learn Latin to work here."

We have another saying that's not as old: "Be ready for anything." That means you must be ready to spot oddness when it strikes. Even if it is something very simPle, like an oversize capital letter in the middle of a word. Did you catch that one? Nice work.

Your first step on an odd case is simple: Just ask, "What seems to be the problem?" But sometimes it's hard to know what to ask after that. Or maybe the person with the odd problem can't tell you. So feel free to use the questions on the next page. We've also included answers from an actual case. We have changed the person's middle name to protect their identity.

22 + 33 + 44 = 99

NAME: Peter Honeytoes Galea | **AGE:** 45

WHAT SEEMS TO BE THE PROBLEM?

I think I'm mostly a goat now. I have human hands, but from the wrists up I'm very hairy, and I smell sort of goat-y. No, I'm going to say very goat-y. When I try to speak I make a goat sound. I also have a tail. You know what, it's easier if I just draw it:

WHEN DID THIS HAPPEN?

Right after breakfast. I don't know the exact time because I couldn't see my watch through all the goat hair.

WHAT WERE YOU DOING WHEN THIS HAPPENED?

The dishes.

Years in a century = 100

DO YOU KNOW WHAT CAUSED THIS TO HAPPEN?

Now that I think of it, I did have seven pounds of goat cheese for breakfast.

DESCRIBE HOW YOU ARE FEELING:

A little nervous, because I'm usually a person. I don't know what life as a goat will be like if I stay this way. Will I be good at my job? I'm an accountant, so I work a lot with important papers and I'm afraid I might chew them up. It has been hard not to chew this questionnaire.

HAVE YOU EVER CONTACTED ODD SQUAD BEFORE?

Once. But by accident. I was trying to call a pizza place to order a goat cheese pizza. Hmm, I may have a goat cheese problem.

DO WE HAVE PERMISSION TO USE GADGETS?

Yes. If you have a hay-inator, please use that first. I am very hungry.

DO WE HAVE PERMISSION TO BRING YOU TO HEADQUARTERS?

Yes. You also have permission to bring me to a farm if that's easier. Or a petting zoo. That always seemed like a pleasant life for a goat.

EMERGENCY CONTACT:

My wife. She's standing right next to me. She's the one who is also mostly a goat.

WHAT'S REALLY ODD WITH THIS PICTURE?

This floating woman seems odd, but an agent would notice she's wearing a tiny but effective jet pack. The odd thing about this woman is that her name is Carol, but she really, really looks like a Susan.

Upside-down family—odd, right? Wrong. This is just the Bouffard family balancing on their heads for fun. What *is* odd is that their picnic blanket just switched from polka dots to checkered. It's too bad you missed the polka dot version. It looked way better.

24 + 25 + 26 + 27 = 102

While a dog walking a man seems odd, on closer inspection an agent would realize that this dog is Kelvin M. Hecklemeyer, the smartest schnauzer on Earth. So not that odd. What *is* odd is that Kelvin is also walking an invisible cheetah.

This may look like a normal toy car, but a sharp agent will realize it's actually a shrunken car driven by two tiny villains. The clue? A very small glove was dropped by the driver's-side door. See it? Hey, nobody said this job would be easy.

Creature attack! False alarm. Just a kid on the way to a costume party. The odd thing is that the kid behind the mask is from the future.

34 + 34 + 34 + 1 = 103

FORM O-135

After solving a case, please fill out the following form and submit it to your Mr. or Ms. O.

TO BE FILLED OUT BY AGENT

Name: Olive | Badge Number: 63 | Partner: Otto

Case Assigned By: Ms. O, Precinct #13579

Time Started: December 24, four o'clock in the afternoon | Time Finished: December 25, daybreak (all over the world)

Odd Problem: Santa's reindeer were accidentally shrunk and escaped from the North Pole.

Villains Encountered on Case (if applicable): None

Evidence Gathered: Contacted Odd Squad agents all over the world to help spot the tiny reindeer. | Gadgets Used: Shrink-inator (see above); grow-inator (once reindeer were found)

Solution to Problem: With the help of a grid, my partner and I were able to figure out that the escaped reindeer were traveling in a shape pattern. Once we cracked the different shape patterns, we were able to predict where the reindeer were headed next. Agents across the world captured the tiny reindeer and sent them back to us at the North Pole. Once the tiny reindeer arrived, we regrew them. We then high-fived.

Meals or Snacks Enjoyed on Case: Candy canes, eggnog, gingerbread

Is there anything else Odd Squad should know about this case?: For a short time, my partner and I became mini Santa Clauses with real beards.

401 backward = 104

FORM O-135

TO BE FILLED OUT BY PERSON WITH ODD PROBLEM

Name: **Santa Claus**

How satisfied are you with Odd Squad's service?
☐ not satisfied   ☐ somewhat satisfied   ☐ satisfied
☑ extremely satisfied

How likely are you to recommend Odd Squad to a friend?
☐ not likely   ☐ somewhat likely   ☐ likely   ☑ extremely likely

Did the Odd Squad agent ask you "What seems to be the problem?"
and address you as "sir" or "ma'am"?
☐ yes   ☑ no **(They called me Santa Claus because I am Santa Claus.)**

Did the agent correctly and promptly diagnose your odd problem?
☑ yes   ☐ no

Which of the following adjectives would you use to describe the
agent that assisted you?

☑ Courteous   ☑ Bright   ☐ Pushy   ☑ Tall
                                          **(but I mostly hang
☑ Friendly   ☑ Professional   ☐ Ineffective   around with elves)**

Are there any other comments you wish to share about your
experience with Odd Squad?

Ho, ho, ho!

100 + 1 + 1 + 1 + 1 + 1 = 105

SERIES

XII

WE INTERRUPT THIS BOOK FOR

WHY ORCHID? WHY NOW? ORCHID NOW

What's up, Shermans? My name is Agent Orchid. Welcome to my section of the handbook. Why do I get my own section? Funny story:

When I was asked to join Odd Squad I agreed under one condition: If there was ever an agent's handbook, I would get four pages to do whatever I want. The bosses said, "Yeah, sure, no problem." They thought they'd NEVER make a handbook. Well . . . here we are! And who's laughing now? I am!

Let's get this Sherman started.

ORCHID'S GUIDE TO MAKING A GREAT SAND CASTLE

1. Get some sand. I hope you knew this part.

2. Get tools. Shovels, pails, that kind of thing.

3. Have lots of water nearby. You need wet sand, Shermans.

4. Build a strong foundation and whack it with your shovel.

5. Start building a tower, using your biggest buckets first.

6. Make it amazing.

FAVORITE WAYS I WRITE MY NAME

Orchid   Orquídea   Ore-Kid   dihcrO   ORCH!D

FAVORITE EXTINCT ANIMAL	FAVORITE NON-EXTINCT ANIMAL

A duck. Mostly because I like the look on Agent Otis's face when I show him one.

7 + 100 - 7 + 7 - 100 + 100 = 107

2 + 2 + 50 + 50 + 2 + 2 = 108

FAVORITE MAGIC TRICK

1. Pick a number.
2. Double it.
3. Add 9.
4. Subtract 3.
5. Divide by 2.
6. Subtract your original number.

The answer is always 3!

FAVORITE OPTICAL ILLUSION

* Shermans! Look at this incredible optical illusion somebody showed me. Which line do you think is longer? Look at them first and then I'll tell you the answer.

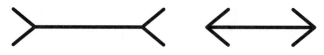

* They're the same length! Isn't that incredible?

FAVORITE NUMBER = 40

Because it's the only number that is spelled with its letters all in alphabetical order: forty. Makes you mad at all the other numbers, doesn't it?

FAVORITE TONGUE TWISTER *

❦ OLD OLLIE OILS OILY OTTERS. ❧

Try saying that ten times fast, Sherman.

1 + 108 = 109

CHUNK

XIII

TUBE TRAVEL

A gent O'Malley here. I run the tube lobby in Precinct #13579. Actually, I share the job with tube operators O'Flynn, O'Ida, O'Neil, O'Dennis, O'Toole, O'Hara, O'Edward, O'Malley, O'Argyle, O'Nancy, O'Edgar, O'Woodruff, O'Higgins, O'Oakley, O'Brady, O'Bill, O'Yancy, O'Leary, O'Ian, O'Kelly, O'Earl, O'Tatum, O'Edwin, O'Nevins, O'Nay, O'Innis, O'Shea, plus a bunch of other tube operators who didn't want their names printed in this handbook.

In case you were wondering, we each work seven-minute shifts every nine weeks. Whew, the schedule is brutal.

To get the next villain tip, look at the other tube operators O'Malley mentions. The second letter of each name will spell out an important way to distract villains from creating oddness. Then turn to page 151 for the next tip.

40 + 30 + 20 + 10 + 10 = 110

So what is the tube system? The Odd Squad tube system is a bunch of tubes.

Hi. O'Malley here again. I turned in my handbook section into the guy in charge of the handbook stuff, Agent Omorro, and he said I had to explain more. Here goes:

The Odd Squad tube system is a bunch of tubes that go around the world.

Hi. O'Malley here AGAIN. Agent Omorro said I still had to explain the tubes better. How is this?

The Odd Squad tube system is a complex series of subterranean and terranean interconnected polyethylene cylinders used to transport professionally dressed juvenile humans anywhere in the world.

Now Agent Omorro said it was too complicated. Man, he will NEVER be satisfied. Look, the tubes get you where you need to go. And if you want to know more about them, that's what the next few pages are for. ARE YOU HAPPY NOW, OMORRO?

Hi. O'Malley here one last time. Agent Omorro said he is happy.

Sincerely,

O'Malley

Agent O'Malley

3 ones standing next to each other = 111

HOW TO RIDE IN THE TUBES

Find your tube lobby. The whole rest of this thing won't work if you don't do this step.

Enter an empty tube.

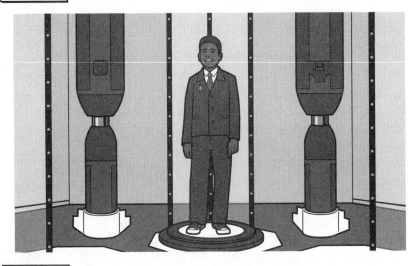

STEP 3 Tell your tube operator where you would like to go.

100 + a dozen = 112

Prepare to squishinate by ducking down into a comfortable position.

Squishinate!

100 + a baker's dozen = 113

Whoosh through the tubes.

Arrive at your destination.

NOTE: There is no drawing for this because you didn't tell us where you were going.

TIPS FOR NERVOUS TUBE TRAVELERS

While most kids enjoy tube travel, some kids get nervous being squished into a ball and whipped around the world at 45,000 miles per hour. If this is you, here are some tips to make tube travel more enjoyable:

1. **TIME.** Give yourself enough time to get to the tube lobby. If you rush, you might get sweaty and then you will slip and slide inside your squished ball.

2. **STAY BUSY.** Bring activities to do during tube travel. Unfortunately, the tubes move so fast, you will probably only be traveling for a few seconds. So make sure you have very short games ready like drawing half a circle, or naming all the planets you live on.

3. **FOOD AND DRINKS TO AVOID.** Avoid all food and drinks.

4. **BREATHE.** Breathe in and out through your mouth or your nose. If you try breathing in or out somewhere else you will hurt yourself.

5. **SAFETY.** Remind yourself that tube travel is the safest way to travel. If you don't count airplanes and cars and trains and boats and bicycles and scooters and skateboards and horse-drawn wagons and getting shot out of a cannon or going over a waterfall in a barrel . . . Actually, don't remind yourself about any of this. It will just make you more nervous.

5 + 15 + 45 + 50 = 115

FREQUENT ADVERBS USED TO DESCRIBE TUBE TRAVEL

Quickly	Loudly	Boldly
Extremely	Briskly	Efficiently
Wonderfully	Cylindrically	Truly
Briefly	Enjoyably	Madly
Nauseously	Nervously	Deeply

INFREQUENT ADVERBS USED TO DESCRIBE TUBE TRAVEL

Quietcalmandpeacefully

100 + 16 - 100 + 16 - 16 - 100 + 100 + 100 = 116

HOW TO FIND TUBE ENTRANCES

One of your jobs as an agent is to find hidden tube entrances. Can you find the ten tube entrances in this picture? Turn the page for the answer!

9 + 9 + 9 + 90 = 117

181 scrambled sideways = 118

SHOULD I TUBE TRAVEL?

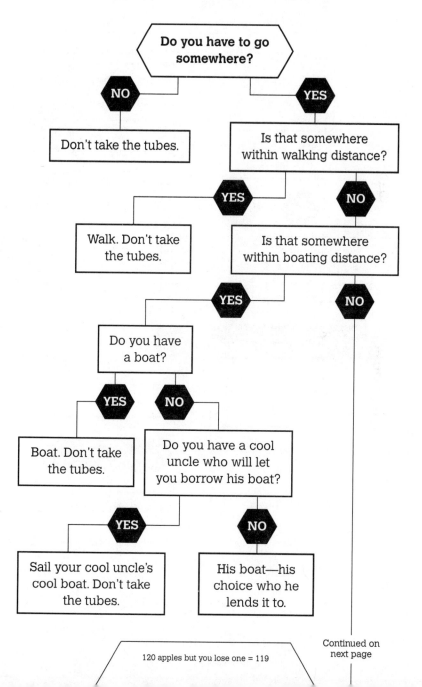

Do you have to go somewhere?

NO → Don't take the tubes.

YES → Is that somewhere within walking distance?

Is that somewhere within walking distance?

YES → Walk. Don't take the tubes.

NO → Is that somewhere within boating distance?

Is that somewhere within boating distance?

YES → Do you have a boat?

NO → *(Continued on next page)*

Do you have a boat?

YES → Boat. Don't take the tubes.

NO → Do you have a cool uncle who will let you borrow his boat?

Do you have a cool uncle who will let you borrow his boat?

YES → Sail your cool uncle's cool boat. Don't take the tubes.

NO → His boat—his choice who he lends it to.

120 apples but you lose one = 119

Continued on next page

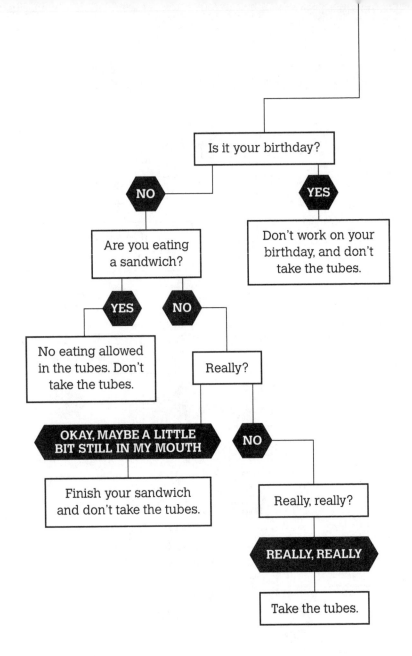

Is it your birthday?

NO → Are you eating a sandwich?

YES → Don't work on your birthday, and don't take the tubes.

Are you eating a sandwich?

YES → No eating allowed in the tubes. Don't take the tubes.

NO → Really?

No eating allowed in the tubes. Don't take the tubes.

OKAY, MAYBE A LITTLE BIT STILL IN MY MOUTH → Finish your sandwich and don't take the tubes.

Really?

NO → Really, really?

Really, really?

REALLY, REALLY → Take the tubes.

stick a zero after 12 = 120

EPISODE

XIV

FITNESS & NUTRITION

AGENTS!

COACH O HERE. I'M USING ALL CAPS SO YOU CAN PICTURE ME
SHOUTING AT YOU. BECAUSE THIS IS IMPORTANT. YOUR BODY IS
LIKE A BATTERY. IF YOU USE IT ALL DAY AND ALL NIGHT IT WILL
GET DEPLETED. AND IT'S NOT THE KIND OF BATTERY YOU CAN
GO BUY AT THE STORE WHEN IT RUNS OUT. IT'S LIKE A FANCY
RECHARGEABLE BATTERY BUT WITH FLESH AND SKIN AND
ORGANS. I'M GLAD THEY DON'T SELL THOSE AT THE STORE. I
WOULDN'T SHOP AT THAT STORE. IT WOULD WEIRD ME OUT.

HOLD ON, I NEED TO DO FOUR HUNDRED SQUATS.

next page after 120 = 121

I'M BACK. WHAT I'M SAYING IS, YOU HAVE TO TAKE CARE OF YOUR BODY. FEED IT. REST IT. AND MOVE IT. ON THE NEXT PAGE ARE SOME EXERCISES TO GET YOU MOVING.

GO, GO, GO! WHEEEEEEEEEEEIIIIT.

THAT WAS ME BLOWING MY WHISTLE. CAME OUT KIND OF WEIRD IN A BOOK.

222 - 100 = 122

COACH O'S EXERCISES TO STAY FIT

PINKIE FINGER CALISTHENICS

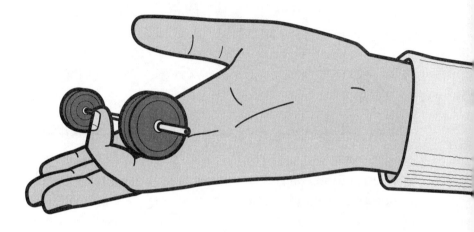

WHY DO IT: It's common for agents to sprain their pinkie, so you need to keep it in tiptop shape. My pinkie can bench press two hundred pounds, and I'm not afraid to brag about it.

YOU'LL NEED: A tiny barbell and your pinkie's favorite music. Every pinkie is different—my left pinkie enjoys disco, but my right pinkie likes jazz.

DO THIS: For one hour make your pinkie jump around and lift the barbell and shout, "Woo! Yeah! I'm a finger!"

TRAINING TIP: To avoid injury, lift with your knuckle, not your fingertip.

smoosh first three numbers together = 123

BRAIN SIT-UPS

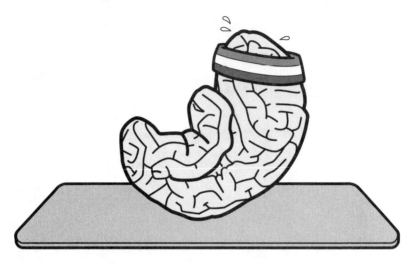

WHY DO IT: If you don't exercise your brain, you'll do not-smart things like forgetting to finish writing a

YOU'LL NEED: Your brain. If you can't find your brain, then borrow one from another agent.

DO THIS: The only way to make your brain sit up is to think about sitting up. You can also think about someone else sitting up, like a cow or an elevator repair person or an elevator repair cow.

TRAINING TIP: To prevent soreness, after your workout spend five minutes thinking about an ice pack.

BLOB WRESTLING

WHY DO IT: Why not?

YOU'LL NEED: A blob who agrees to wrestle with you.
And a pack of napkins.

DO THIS: Wrestle the blob for ten rounds. Whoever wins the
most rounds gets to be the king of Canada for the day.* That last
part just makes it a little more interesting.

TRAINING TIP: When wrestling a blob, never say, "Ew, gross."
That's poor sportsmanship and will hurt the blob's feelings.

Canada does not have a king. That's called a fake out.

25 + 25 + 25 + 25 + 25 = 125

WIN THE WORLD SERIES OF BASEBALL

WHY DO IT: What better way to stay fit and have some fun than to win the World Series of baseball?

YOU'LL NEED: Talent, determination, and the ability to bunt.

DO THIS: Become very good at baseball. Join a professional baseball team. Play so well that your team wins the most games and then triumphs in the World Series.

TRAINING TIP: If your partner asks you where you've been for the last seven months, say, "I've been right here, where have you been?" That'll get 'em thinking.

OKSANA'S GUIDE TO NUTRITION

Hello. My name is Agent Oksana. I make food for the agents of Precinct #13579. Apparently I also write things in books now.

Food is something you put in your mouth and swallow so you can live. Depending on the food, you may have to chew it first. If you have to chew, I suggest using your teeth.

You can bring your own food from home or buy food in the Odd Squad cafeteria. Food in the cafeteria costs nothing, which is a good bargain, if you ask me.

The following is a menu showing the food served in your Odd Squad cafeteria Monday through Friday. Did I have fun making this menu? Judge for yourself.

Here is a photo of me before I made the menu:

And here is a photo of me after I made the menu:

first prime number since 113 = 127

ODD SQUAD MENU

MONDAY

Breakfast: Oatmeal.
Odd Option: Floating Oatmeal.

Snack: Yogurt.
Odd Option: Invisible Yogurt
(same nutritional value).

Lunch: Grilled Cheese.
Odd Option: Grilled Threes
(only three per agent).

Dinner: Pad Thai.
Odd Option: Patio Thai.

TUESDAY

Breakfast: Scrambled Eggs and Toast.
Odd Option: Scrambled Toast with Gregs
(subject to availability of at least two Gregs).

Snack: Peaches in Syrup.
Odd Option: Peaches in Antarctica
(transportation provided).

Lunch: Spaghetti and Meatballs.
Odd Option: Spaghetti and Tiny Meteors.

Dinner: Soup Dumplings.
Odd Option: Circles Inside More Circles
with Circle Sauce.

$64 + 32 + 16 + 8 + 4 + 2 + 1 + 1 = 128$

WEDNESDAY

Breakfast: Dry Cereal.
Odd Option: Wet Blankets.

Snack: Trail Mix.
Odd Option: Highway Mix.

Lunch: Corn Chowder.
Odd Option: Unicorn Chowder
(stirred by unicorns).

Dinner: Tofu Stir Fry.
Odd Option: Stardust
(chopsticks provided).

THURSDAY

Breakfast: Pancakes.
Odd Option: Pancakes from Three Years in the Future
(still pretty much the same, just a little stale).

Snack: Fruit Cup.
Odd Option: Fruit Fifty-Thousand-Seat Stadium.

Lunch: Hard-Shell Taco.
Odd Option: Hard-Shell Taco with Tasteful Wallpaper.

Dinner: Chicken Pot Pie.
Odd Option: One Medium-Size Wish.

FRIDAY

Breakfast: Make Your Own Omelet.
Odd Option: The Omelet Makes You!

Snack: Mixed Nuts.
Odd Option: Mixed Nuts Except the Flavors
Are All Switched Around.

Lunch: French Bread Pizza.
Odd Option: Assorted Piano Keys.

Dinner: Meatloaf.
Odd Option: The Same Meatloaf. But with a
Slightly Different Meatloaf on the Inside.

$$65 + 43 + 21 = 129$$

PROS AND CONS OF POTATOES

By Agent Olaf

I am Olaf. Yay!

If you don't like what is on the lunch menu, I have some good news. There is always an option for potatoes. I like potatoes. They mean so much to me. Do you like potatoes? This list of pros and cons can help you decide whether potatoes are right for you in your heart.

65 twice = 130

PROS	CONS
They taste so good.	
So beautiful. Just look at one.	
So many kinds. Russet, Yukon Gold, Yam, Fingerling, Red Gold. I could go on.	
Grown in the ground. How neat!	
Have eyes but never watch you.	
Vitamin B6 and more potassium than a banana. What? Yes.	
There is a whole potato land with magical potatoes in it.	
Sometimes you can see a face in one.	
Think of all the ways to make them. Baked, mashed, salad, boiled, chips, au gratin. I could go on.	
Okay, I will go on. Latkes, home fries, french fries, hash browns, tots, roasted with herbs, garlic mashed ... uh-oh, I'm out of room. Potato! Ooh, there's a little more room. POTATO!!!!	

second prime number since 113 = 131

WORKPLACE SAFETY

I'm Agent Owen, and I'm head of security. I don't want to say it's the most important job at Odd Squad, but I guess I just said it anyway. I mean, think about it. If villains were able to sneak into headquarters, they could cause all kinds of trouble. I should know, because I've seen it happen a bunch of times. Usually it starts when I go on break. Hey, I never said I was perfect. But I'm close.

It's my job to make sure that Odd Squad is a safe place for you to work. But you have to do your part. I won't always be there to catch you when you fall. Or to stop you from getting that paper cut.

33 + 33 + 33 + 33 = 132

Or to smack away that bowl of way-too-old chili that you definitely shouldn't be eating. Actually, I probably will be there for that last one. It would happen in the break room, and I love that place.

I leave you with a little saying I made up that can help you remember to be safe. Here it is: "Be safe." I didn't say it was a clever phrase, but I think it really does the job.

Speaking of doing the job. . . I've been doing mine for an hour straight and could really use some rest. Going on break!

100 + 11 + 11 + 11 = 133

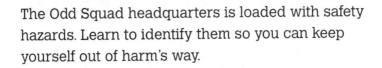

The Odd Squad headquarters is loaded with safety hazards. Learn to identify them so you can keep yourself out of harm's way.

Regular stairs. But just be careful on the stairs. Hold the railing.

Self-driving desk chair.

Held in place with arts and crafts glue.

Sometimes a portal to Blobsylvania.

Between 2:32 P.M. and 2:34 P.M. the sandbox turns into a quicksand box.

45 + 45 + 45 = 135

WATCH OUT FOR EACH OTHER

There are 45,987 kids working in an Odd Squad at any given time. Most of them are invisible. Here are five tips to keep you and your fellow kids safe at work.

1. When putting on a backpack, make sure it is a backpack and not the arms and body of an agent.

2. When playing basketball, make sure it is a ball and not an agent's body curled up in a ball.

34 + 17 + 34 + 17 + 34 = 136

3. When walking, make sure it is on the ground and not on the body of an agent.

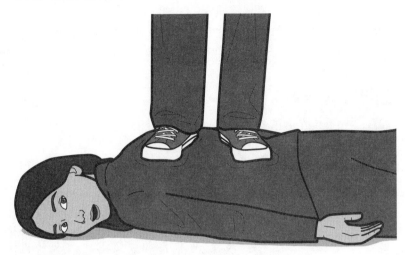

4. When tying your shoes, make sure it is shoelaces and not fingers on an agent's hand.

5. When biting into a sandwich, make sure it is a sandwich and not an agent's head between two slices of bread.

100 + 30 + 7 = 137

SAFE VS. UNSAFE

There are two ways to do every activity at Odd Squad: the safe way and the unsafe way. Always choose the safe way.

USING A PEN

SAFE: Pen taped to the agent's hand so agent won't lose it.

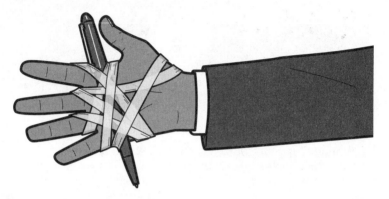

UNSAFE: Pen not taped. Also, agent on edge of cliff.

CHOOSING YOUR DESK

SAFE: Desk has four sturdy legs.

UNSAFE: Only three legs on desk. And on an airplane in the sky.

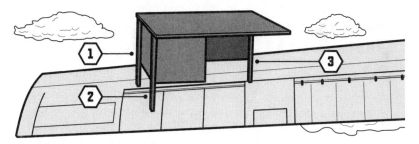

MAKING A PHONE CALL

SAFE: Agent seated safely at desk, free of distractions.

UNSAFE: Do we even need to explain this one?

QUESTIONS & ANSWERS

This part of the handbook has questions, and also answers. What is a question? That was a question. What is an answer? This is an answer.

We'll be honest, we don't have much else to say to introduce this part of the handbook. It kind of speaks for itself. But if we stop writing this introduction right now, there will be a big, empty white space at the bottom of the page. So we're going to include a few more sentences. What will they be about? We don't know, because we are writing them right now.

Oh, hey, we just figured out a way to fill the rest of the empty page. We can just quote ourselves! Like we said, "This part of the handbook has questions, and also answers. What is a question? That was a question. What is an answer? This is an answer."

FREQUENTLY ASKED QUESTIONS ABOUT ODD SQUAD

What if my name doesn't start with *O*? Can I still be in Odd Squad?

Of course. If you don't have an *O* name you'll be assigned one on your first day at headquarters.

But I like my name. It's Alexander!

Hi, Alexander. We will try to keep most of your regular name. Your Odd Squad name would be Olexander.

Why do Odd Squad agents wear suits?

We are a professional organization, so it's important to look professional.

Then why do agents wear sneakers?

Ever try chasing a creature in penny loafers? So many blisters.

What's the different between weird and odd?

A propeller hat is weird. A propeller hat on a floating head is odd.

What is the difference between strange and odd?

Strange and odd have none of the same letters and also sound different when you say them.

Can any kid join Odd Squad?

Yes. Agents can join as early as one second old. Earlier than that takes too much training.

You say that Agent Oscar invented the science department only a few years ago, but I saw a picture of Odd Squad scientists in

the Old West. Also, I saw a photo of Agent Oscar as a kid wearing a lab coat. How is this possible?

Time travel.

Why do tube operators and maintenance workers have the same department symbol?

Kids in each department thought of the shape at the exact same time, and we didn't want to disappoint anyone.

Can adults join Odd Squad?

For the last time, Ms. Williamson, no, they may not. Odd Squad is an organization run entirely by kids.

Why is Odd Squad run by kids and not adults?

Hello again, Ms. Williamson. Odd Squad has found that adults often get freaked out by odd things. Kids, on the other hand, take the oddness in stride.

What is the best part of working at Odd Squad?

There's no right answer to this question. But the most right answer is the joy of working on a team to do something good.

What if an adult is really young at heart? Could that adult join Odd Squad?

Hi again, Ms. Williamson.

Hi. Thought I'd sneak that one by you.

Odd Squad catches everything. Also, that wasn't a question.

What is the most frequently asked of the frequently asked questions?

That one, actually.

71 + 71 = 142

INFREQUENTLY ASKED QUESTIONS ABOUT ODD SQUAD

Is it okay to say the word "slacks" while riding in the tubes?

Of course.

Does Odd Squad have a middle name?

No.

How many jelly beans could you fit in an Odd Squad headquarters?

63 billion last time we tried.

If Odd Squad were an animal what animal would it be?

An ocelot.

Can an Odd Squad headquarters be rented out for birthday parties?

Only by unicorns.

Is there an Odd Squad hopscotch team?

No, but you could start one. Go see your Coach O.

Was Odd Squad ever called "Jerry's House of Weird Stuff"?

Yes.

Is the Odd Squad suit wrinkle-free?

The left side is.

Can I wear a neon green suit instead?

Sure! But not when you're at work.

What is the official flower of Odd Squad?

We don't have one, but Orchid told us we have to say "orchid." So, orchid.

If the Odd Squad ringtone had words, what would they be?

"Your phone is ringing! Your phone is ringing right now! You should answer your phone now!"

Can I bring my llama to work?

Yes.

What happens if I blast something with an Upside-down-inator, then blast the same thing again, and then one more time, and then one more time?

Your lab director will take the upside-down-inator away from you.

Has there ever been a camel in an Odd Squad headquarters?

There have been thirty-four camels in twenty-one different headquarters.

Has there ever been a camel in an Odd Squad headquarters?

This is starting to become a frequently asked question.

Can a Hydroclops survive out of water?

Sure, but it won't be living its best life.

If you took all the balls out of the ball pit would it still be a ball pit?

You just blew my mind.

What is Odd Squad spelled backward spelled backward?

Odd Squad.

36 + 36 + 36 + 36 = 144

ODD SQUAD
HOLIDAYS OBSERVED

Here is a list of official Odd Squad holidays.

JANUARY 2
Jackalope Appreciation Day
(Day Off)

JANUARY 8
Friends of Odd Squad Day
(Day Off for Your Friends Only)

JANUARY 22
Clean Your Badge Day
(Day Off So You Can Take the
Time to Do It Right)

FEBRUARY 18
Everybody Invisible Day
(Day Off Since We Can't See If
You Came to Work Anyway)

FEBRUARY 26
Unreturned Gadget Day
(No Day Off Unless You Return
That Gadget)

MARCH 14
Pi Day (3.14 Days Off)

MARCH 31
March 31st Day (Day Off to
Recover from All That Marching)

APRIL 1
April Fools Day (Day Off) (Just
Kidding, It's Not a Day Off. Get to
Work. April Fools.)

APRIL 21
Villain Unappreciation Day
(Extra Day of Work Added)

MAY 6
Happy Cheer Day (Time Off for
as Long as It Takes to Give a
Happy Cheer)

MAY 10
Juice Box Safety Day (All-Day
Training at Precinct #13579, Ms.
O's office)

MAY 11
Third Holiday in May Day (The
Rest of Month of May Off)

1 + 2 + 3 + 4 + 9 + 18 + 36 + 72 = 145

JUNE 1
Daniel Berryman Awareness Minute (the Minute Between 11:23 A.M. and 11:24 A.M. Off)

JUNE 15
O Games (Day Off)

JUNE 29
Other Earth Day (Day Off on Other Earth Only)

JUNE 30
Go Fly a Kite Day (Day Off for Kite Owners Only)

JULY 10
July Doesn't Have Any Official Odd Squad Holidays Day (Day Off)

AUGUST 1
Partner Appreciation Day (Day Off Plus an Extra Little Bit to Make It Extra Special)

AUGUST 9
August 8th Remembrance Day (No Day Off)

AUGUST 17
Pienado Preparedness Day (All-Day Training at Nearest Cream Pie Factory)

SEPTEMBER 1
Soundcheck: The Band: The Holiday (Three to Five Minutes Off to Enjoy Your Favorite Soundcheck Song)

SEPTEMBER 2
Timetastrophe Savings Time (Bow Before the Time Sheep for as Long as They Want You To)

OCTOBER 4
Oddtoberfest (Day Off)

NOVEMBER
Potato Day (Olaf-Only Day Off)

NOVEMBER 20
Oddsgiving (Give Someone Else the Day Off)

DECEMBER 1
New Year's Eve Eve Eve Eve Eve Eve Eve Eve Eve Eve Eve Eve (Of Course You Get a Day Off for This. What Are We, Monsters?)

GOODBYE LETTER FROM MS. O

Greetings, agent, and congratulations on finishing the *Agent's Handbook*. Unless you didn't finish reading and just flipped to the end. If you did that, congratulations on being smart and double-checking that this book has an ending. That's the worst, when books don't have endings and just stop midsentence like

For those of you who did read the whole handbook, you should now know everything you need to protect the world from oddness. And now that you know everything, you will be a perfect agent and never ever make a mistake.

Sorry. That's not going to happen.

You will make mistakes. Sometimes lots of them. I know I did back when I was an agent. And I still make mistakes now as Ms. O. But there is something else you should know about me. I'm going to write it in small letters so you have to get close to read so it feels like I'm telling you a secret:

Every time I made a mistake, I learned something.

The truth is, if I didn't make those mistakes, I wouldn't have turned into the fabulous person I am today. And I am pretty fabulous. There is one important thing to remember when you do fail. I'm going to write it in big letters so you can't miss it:

DON'T GIVE UP.

49 + 49 + 49 = 147

That goes for Odd Squad. But it also goes for everything else that you care about outside of work. If you have a dream, go for it. You will succeed. How do I know? Easy—Odd Squad has time travel. I've seen your future, and it's so bright it's blinding.

As for now, thanks for protecting the world from oddness.

With even more
appreciation than
before,

Sincerely,

Ms. O

147's next-door neighbor = 148

APPENDIX

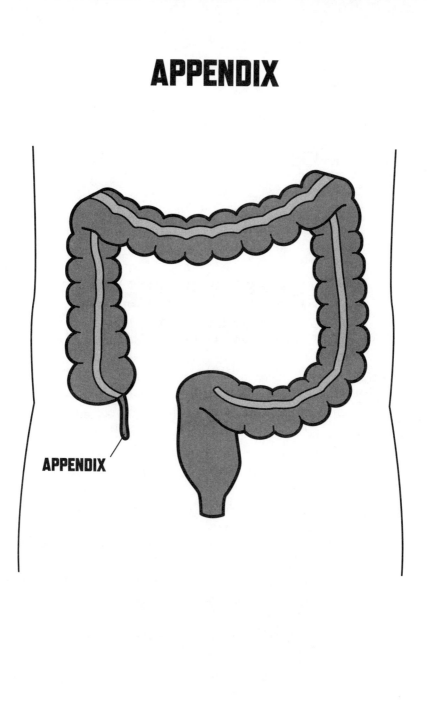

APPENDIX

last prime number before 150 = 149

A PAGE IN ANCIENT JACKALOPIAN

Odd Squad bylaw 3791 says that at least one page of the *Odd Squad Agent's Handbook* must be written in Ancient Jackalopian, which is the language spoken by the original Odd Squad agents. This is that page.

PUBLISHER'S NOTE FROM AGENT OMORRO

On behalf of everyone in the Odd Squad book publishing department, which is just me, thank you for reading this handbook. It took 18 billion days to make. But I also took a lot of long lunches. If you still have 777 million questions about Odd Squad, please read the handbook 632,000 more times. If you do that and still have at least 435 questions, please call the Odd Squad toll-free number. That phone number can be found by adding up the numbers in this paragraph.

Yours always,

Omorro

Omorro

To get your last villain tip, translate this Ancient Jackalopian message. How? There are twenty-six symbols at the top of the previous page. The first one stands for the letter A. The last one stands for the letter Z. The rest of the letters are in order. Now you should know which symbol stands for which letter.

add 1 to previous page = 151

ABOUT THE AUTHORS

TIM MCKEON is a five-time Emmy-winning writer. He is co-creator and head writer for the PBS KIDS series *Odd Squad* and creator of the Apple TV+ series *Helpsters*. He grew up in Westborough, Massachusetts, the hometown of Adam Peltzman.

ADAM PELTZMAN is a five-time Emmy-winning writer. He is co-creator of the PBS KIDS series *Odd Squad* and creator of the Nickelodeon series *Wallykazam!* Adam grew up in Westborough, Massachusetts, the hometown of Tim McKeon.

Top photo: McKeon Family and Sinking Ship Entertainment Inc.
Bottom photo: Peltzman Family and Sinking Ship Entertainment Inc.